Long Legs Boy

"There's so much love and longing in Madison's pages that readers may find their mood suddenly growing mysteriously melancholic..."
BC Bookworld, review of *The Moon's Fireflies*

Long Legs Boy

by

Benjamin Madison

OOLICHAN BOOKS
FERNIE, BRITISH COLUMBIA, CANADA
2012

Library and Archives Canada Cataloguing in Publication

Madison, Benjamin

    Long legs boy / Benjamin Madison.

ISBN 978-0-88982-290-0

    I. Title.

PS8626.A33L65 2012   C813'.6   C2012-907050-5

We gratefully acknowledge the financial support of the Canada Council for
the Arts, the British Columbia Arts Council through the BC Ministry of
Tourism, Culture, and the Arts, and the Government of Canada through
the Canada Book Fund, for our publishing activities.

Published by
Oolichan Books
P.O. Box 2278
Fernie, British Columbia
Canada V0B 1M0

www.oolichan.com

This book is dedicated to Street Children.
Their remarkable spirit has inspired me ever since my first
meeting with them many years ago. It is also dedicated to
those individuals and agencies that give Street Children the
respect that they deserve and the loving care that is theirs
by right as children.

Author's Note

Long Legs Boy is a work of fiction. All people, organizations, places and events in this story are products of the author's imagination. Any resemblance to a real person, organization or agency, a real country or city or to an actual event is purely coincidental and unintentional.

The story of *Long Legs Boy* is set in Africa but Dazania is a completely fictional country and is not modeled after or meant to suggest any specific African country. Aside from small details, Modou's experiences in the streets would be familiar to the street children not only of Africa but of many countries in Asia, the Americas and Europe.

A portion of the income from the sale of this book will be donated to organizations assisting Street Children. If you wish further information please contact Oolichan Books at *info@oolichan.com*.

One

The boy squatted on his heels in the doorway of the mud hut. His chin rested on his crossed forearms and he gazed inertly at the pale, ocher sky. His dark eyes were set in a face that had been sharpened by hunger and sorrow. The cold breeze worried some dry leaves and the dust of *harmattan*, blown south from the Sahara, itched in his nostrils. The fine, reddish grit coated the straw thatch of the village houses like rust and settled on the bare branches of the baobab tree that towered over them. The boy heard rustling on the worn grass mat within the hut.

"Modou."

He went inside and knelt by the mat. His mother's eyes opened.

"Go to Alhaji Safo at Kafabolo," she said.

"We'll go when you get better."

"Go now. I'll come later."

"Mama."

"There is nothing you can do for me. We're all dead now. But I'll rest more easily if...." She choked. Tears glistened in the dusty wrinkles around her eyes, then trickled slowly down cheeks hollowed by the wasting disease that had emptied their village. "Oh, my long legs boy!" she cried and her love poured out of her eyes for the last time.

"Mama," said the boy, but there was no answer.

He wept at her side through the night. In the cold morning he took a mattock to dig her grave beside the house. Four silent mounds were there already, his father, his two sisters and his baby brother. The baked red earth was hard and he was weak from days when there had been little food.

Long shadows crept across the compound before he finished heaping the dry soil. When darkness fell, he lay alone for the first time in his twelve years of life and heard only the scratching and scurrying of lizards in the thatch overhead.

With the dawn's earliest light he set out across the fields toward Kafabolo. The village was silent behind him but the silence was like a long low moan that followed him and twisted inside his heart. He came at noon to another small village.

"Come and eat," said the woman. He buried his face beneath her arms and wept.

"Where are you going?" she asked when he had eaten.

"Alhaji Safo."

"The *marabout*," she said, nodding. "That is good. He has many boys in his *darra* and he is a great teacher. You will eat and you will learn."

"How far is it?"

"It's a little bit far, but if you cross the hills there," she said, pointing, "you'll come to my sister's village. Her name is Kumba. Tell her Safi is well and sends her greetings."

She watched as the boy trudged toward the hills. "Go with God!" she called.

Four days he walked as if asleep. He passed from village to village and the villagers shared their simple meals with him and pointed out the path. Sometimes tears filled his eyes and he stumbled blindly, bruising his bare feet on the rocky track. Then he forced himself to run until he found release in exhaustion. On the fifth day he stood outside the compound of Alhaji Safo. It consisted of a half dozen round huts made of red mud bricks and plastered smooth with the same substance. They were roofed with straw in shades of gold or silver depending on the age of the thatch, but all were now brown with the dust of *harmattan*. The huts were grouped around a large open space. The hard packed earth of the compound yard had been smoothed by the traffic of bare feet and worn to a light tan color by daily sweepings.

The Alhaji and his wife, the Hajiya, and their youngest daughter, Mariama, lived in the largest house. It alone was divided into two rooms so the Alhaji and his wife could sleep in privacy. Adjacent to their house was the kitchen and food storage hut, in front of which were large, three-legged pots and wooden mortars and pestles used in food preparation. Beside the cooking house was the next largest dwelling, that of the Alhaji's nephew, who had chosen to make his life with the *marabout* because he loved him and respected his wisdom. The nephew lived there with his wife and three young children.

On the other side of the Alhaji's house, a knee-high wall defined a clean-swept, rectangular prayer area oriented to face Mecca. Other huts held agricultural implements and what remained of the previous season's harvest. At the opposite end to the Alhaji's dwelling was the boys' house where the *talibés,* the Alhaji's students lived, eight boys ranging in age from eight to sixteen. Beside this, the smallest hut and an attached pen were occupied at night by a dozen goats. A wall of straw mats joined the outer edges of the huts to each other and enclosed the central compound yard. Outside the wall was a well and near it grew five swollen-trunked baobab trees like a neighboring family.

Above the entrance to the Alhaji's house, the thatch extended to shade a porch where the Alhaji liked to sit with his wife. While they relaxed there enjoying the peace of the evening a boy's face peered uncertainly around one of the huts at the other end of the compound. Modou had arrived.

"Aieee," complained the Hajiya in a low voice when she noticed the boy. "Another boy. We have no need of another boy. We can hardly feed those we have."

"Allah sends them," said the Alhaji and called out, "You are welcome, boy. Come. Sit down here. You must be thirsty." He shouted for Mariama to bring some water. When the boy had drunk his fill the Alhaji said, "What is your name?"

"Sheikh Momodou Diallo. They call me Modou."

"Your village?"

"Selongwe. Near Satonga." His voice faltered, "But there is no-one there now."

"No-one?"

"No. All are dead, from the wasting disease."

"Aiee," groaned the Alhaji. "This is very bad. Your father?"

"Alieu Diallo, son of Sheikh Omar Diallo. But all my family are dead."

"I knew your grandfather. He was a good man."

"My mother said I should come to you."

"You are welcome," said Alhaji Safo and shouted for his most senior student. When he came from the boys' hut the

Alhaji instructed him, "Idi, take this boy with you until it's time to eat. Then show him where to sleep."

"He will eat a lot, that one!" said the Hajiya, watching the boys as they moved across the compound. Then she added in a gentler voice, "Such a small boy and so thin, those long legs like sticks."

"A boy without a family, no parents, not one cousin, not one aunt, his brothers and sisters all dead. I pray we are never so alone as he." Alhaji Safo fingered his wooden prayer beads and intoned in a low voice a few suras from the Holy Koran. "This will either kill him or put iron in his soul," he said.

"It must have taken him four or five days to walk here," said the Hajiya. "I think he will live."

"Insh'Allah," said the Alhaji and repeated another verse from the Koran.

"Insh'Allah," echoed the Hajiya.

"Wife, let us kill a chicken for him. I saw something in his eyes."

"Yes, but not tonight. He's still floating. When he comes to earth, perhaps in a few days. Tonight our chicken would feed only ghosts."

"I know every sura in the Holy Koran, my dear, but you are a scholar of the heart."

In the morning, Modou awoke before light when he heard the rhythmic thump of the pestle pounding the day's *coos* grains for the morning meal. For an instant, he dreamed he was in his village with his family and that it was his mother making breakfast. Then he saw his mind pulling him toward this dream to make him sad, inviting him to feel sorry for himself. On his journey, he had walked in a grief sometimes so heavy he had wanted only to collapse and die beside the path. He had fought this temptation then, seeing it as a trap where, if he chose, he could dwell in pain forever. He closed the door to the past and resolutely opened his eyes to meet the new day.

"Come," said the boy who had slept beside him on the mat. "Let us go and make ablutions before we pray. Then we will learn. And then, we will eat. After that we will work. That is how we do here."

The days passed and the healing rhythm of sleep and prayer and work wove those days into weeks and months. Modou grew stronger. His work during *harmattan* was to care for the Alhaji's goats. Each day he and several other boys took them to the river to drink and to browse among the shrubs and trees that lined its banks.

One day, an *mbarodi*, a spotted hyena, came slinking from behind the boulders on the riverbank, sidling toward a newborn kid. The boys threw stones and chased it away. For three days it returned, sneaking through the bush and making its hateful crazy noises when struck by their missiles. Then it went away. Aside from protecting the goats from such threats and keeping them from straying, the days were peaceful and the boys played in the river's cool shallows while the goats nibbled the leaves from the low growth that clustered at its edges.

In the early morning, after the mid-day meal and in the evening, the Alhaji taught the boys suras from the Koran. They copied each verse on tombstone-shaped, wooden tablets called *aluyeh* and repeated the verse until they could read it easily and recite it from memory. The pens they used were made from a kind of grass that grew near the river and had only to be cut to the proper length and sharpened before use. Idi taught Modou how to make *darha*, the washable black ink. They scraped the soot from the Hajiya's cooking pots and boiled it with water and sugar to make it thick and sticky.

Every day the boys collected firewood for cooking and for the Alhaji's night lessons. Men and women from neighboring compounds trekked across the fields with their children to attend these and sat around the fire to learn from the Alhaji. After the lesson there was talk and often, storytelling. The boys stayed up then until the bright stars swam in the velvet sky. As they drifted into sleep, Arabic verses mingled in their minds with the wondrous doings of magical animals. In the boys' dreams, the great Tijani *marabouts* of jihads long past marched again through the mists on the Futa Jalon plateau.

Modou's application to his Koranic studies pleased Alhaji Safo. The boy was eager and quick to learn. After the lesson one afternoon the marabout noticed Modou and some other boys bent over a sandy patch in the compound. Modou was writing with a stick in the sand, "A B C D E F G."

"And so you are a teacher too," said the Alhaji.

"I'm sorry, *Cherno*," said Modou, using the respectful form of address that meant teacher. "I was just showing them some letters. I learned writing when I went to school near our village."

"But that's not Arabic writing. That's English."

"Yes, but it's the same, only different shapes." Modou remembered how the *marabout* sometimes warned them of the Satan of the West and the wickedness of America, where lewd behavior and killing were normal. "I know it's not holy, like the Koran."

"No. It is not holy. But it's knowledge and it is to be

respected. Knowledge is never evil. It's what people do with it that makes it evil or good. How long were you in school?"

"I went three years, when my mother was able to pay the fees."

"And you can speak English as well as write it?"

"Better, *Cherno*. English is not difficult to speak but the writing is harder than Arabic. Sometimes a letter has one sound and sometimes it has another sound. It's very hard to put the letters into words correctly."

Some days after their lessons the boys would go to the river to wash their clothes and swim. Other times they would play with a football made from old plastic slippers bound and melted together to make a sphere. With nine boys in the compound there were good games. When the Hajiya complained about their noise the Alhaji said, "Boys need to play and make noise. That's how they grow."

"Are we raising giants then? Aieee! My head is ringing."

The Alhaji nodded, and then told the boys to go and play in the fields outside the compound.

The *harmattan* season ended and the wind from the south blew the dust from the sky. This was the hottest season of the year, the time before the rains when the sky felt like a headache, a heavy pressure behind the eyes. The air thickened and plump clouds piled up on the horizon. The Alhaji borrowed a donkey to pull his old plough. There was much work to do preparing the fields and sowing the seed so that when the rainy season arrived all would be ready. Then the *coos* and groundnuts would spring up and cover the reddish fields with luminous green. Everyone worked all morning. After lunch they returned to the fields and labored until it was too dark to continue.

The rains began one afternoon while they were resting

after their mid-day meal. There came a little wind, deliciously fresh and moist. Then the sky filled with great dark clouds and large drops spattered in the dust, the first rain in nine months. The boys ran from their hut into the compound and raised their arms and faces to the sky. As the rain increased they capered around to the rear of their hut, threw off their clothes and stood under the eaves to let the cool runoff splash over their naked bodies while they slapped their feet happily in the mud. The air was light and rich with moisture and they ran wildly over the fields, turning cartwheels and shouting and spinning in joy.

The thirsty earth drank up the water and it was possible to rest a little in the evening while seed and soil and water performed their ancient alchemy. When the weeds sprouted, everyone would again be bent over their hoes all day and under the moon, but now they could have a brief respite and enjoy the coolness before nightfall.

The Hajiya fenced a plot near the riverside and planted a garden of tomatoes, peppers, garden eggs and other vegetables. Often in the afternoon when the others had gone to the fields she took Modou to help her with this small garden. Modou loved to cultivate these plants and he and the Hajiya worked together in quiet contentment.

As the shadows stretched across the compound yard one evening, the Alhaji and his wife sat in front of their house and watched the boys playing football.

"That Modou is a good worker," said the Hajiya. "No matter what you ask him to do he always does it with a smile and does it well and carefully."

"Yes, he's very good," agreed the Alhaji. "And look at him run. I'm getting to be very old. I can hardly remember what it was like to run like that, and after working all day, too."

"So you were a fast runner when you were a boy?"

"Oh yes, I was, truly! But not like that. You know, I don't have those long legs."

"Oh!" exclaimed the Hajiya. "You've reminded me of something."

"What is it?"

"Three days ago, before lunch, I was scolding the boys because the firewood was wet."

"Yes, you have a sharp tongue, my dear."

"And Modou was there and you know, I particularly like to scold him because he can always make me laugh. No matter what complaint I make he turns it to a joke somehow, so sometimes I scold him just to feel better."

"Yes, I've seen that. He's the only boy who understands that when you scold, it's just play."

"Not always. Sometimes I have good reason to be angry, although I don't think I've ever been really angry with Modou."

She paused.

"Yes, my dear?"

"What you said about long legs reminded me. I was scolding Modou and he was looking very serious but laughing with his eyes the way he does. I was calling him names and then I called him a 'long legs boy' and he turned to look at me. Oh!" She shook her head. "It was just as if I had cut him across the face with a knife. He just ran away. You remember how we found him already working in the field when we returned later in the day."

"I wondered about that."

"I can't forget the look on his face. So much pain. I have been thinking about it. It must have been his mother who called him 'long legs boy.'" She nodded her head emphatically. "Yes. I'm sure that was her pet name for him. It came so easily to my tongue."

They sat quietly, inert with the physical exhaustion resulting from weeks of strenuous labor. The Alhaji murmured verses from the Koran and clicked through his rosary.

"Is that a sin?" she asked, "to cause so much pain without meaning to?"

"No, my dear. How could you know?"

"Aieee. It feels like a sin."

"I'm sure he knows you meant no harm."

"Oh I know he has already forgiven me. That's how good he is. But when I saw that pain, it caused a pain in me too. I'm so foolish. I thought to keep him here with us. But he will not stay. He needs something he cannot find here. He will leave."

"Most children do, my dear. Even our own have left, except for Mariama, but she is too young yet. And all mothers mourn when it happens." He paused. "And fathers too."

When Modou recalled that rainy season, he thought most often of the month when *follereh,* the red sorrel, patched the hillsides with its scarlet blooms. The boys gathered these fleshy flowers and the Hajiya boiled them and sweetened the tart liquid to make the ruby-colored *wanjo,* a beverage so cool and refreshing that it seemed to Modou like a drink from the fountains of paradise.

Several times during this season nomadic Fulas with their herds of cattle and goats passed through the countryside, grazing their animals over the hills and along the riverbanks and carefully avoiding the land where crops were growing. The wandering tribesmen revered the Alhaji and visited him in the evenings to study with him and seek his advice on spiritual matters. They brought with them gifts of butter and calabashes of yogurt. The following mornings the Hajiya pounded the *coos* until it was as fine and light as air, then mixed it with yogurt and sugar to make the thick, nutty-tasting gruel called *latchiry a kossam*. Licking their lips and fingers, the boys agreed there could be no finer food anywhere on earth.

The rains came at the correct time to bring the crops out of the ground but then they failed. Day after day the sun beat down on the young plants and they began to dry out and die. Then the rain fell with fury and at the end of three days' downpour, half the crop that had survived the dry period had been washed out of the soil. What remained grew well until near the harvest. Then the sky darkened and the rain descended in torrents for nearly a week and spoiled much of the maturing crop. After harvest, the Alhaji sold the few bags of groundnuts his fields had yielded and paid the small debts he had incurred buying seed and other agricultural supplies. The harvest provided nearly enough *coos* to feed all in the Alhaji's compound until the following year.

One day early in the dry season the Alhaji returned from the *lumo*, the big weekly market in Kafabalo, where he liked to go to meet old friends and hear the news. When he had finished his prayers, the Hajiya served him his evening meal. After he had eaten his fill, the Hajiya brought him a glass of *booy*, the cooling drink made from the seedpods of the baobab tree.

This was the best time of the year. The rains had finished but there was still a little green on the land and though the days were hot, the evenings were cool and pleasant. The Alhaji sat back contentedly and smiled.

"Today in Kafabalo I saw the father of Idi and Buba."

"You're smiling," said the Hajiya. "Does that mean he wants to take them back to his compound this season? Indeed I doubt we have enough to feed everyone here until next year."

"Oh no, my dear. Better news than that. On his side of the hills they didn't suffer from too much rain as we did. He was very happy with his harvest and very pleased with my teaching of his sons. He said that although he had enough to feed them this year he would rather they stayed with me until their learning was complete. He promised that sometime soon he will bring us some sacks of *coos* and a sack of rice."

"Allah be praised! I was beginning to worry. I have heard that in Kafabolo many young men are leaving for the city now. Some have gone already and more are leaving every day."

"Set your mind at rest, my dear. We will have enough food, this year at least, so that I won't have to take the boys to the city to beg. We'll be able to enjoy your company here until the rains come again."

"Ah!" she laughed. "You're too old to enjoy my company any longer."

"My dear, I pray to have your company forever." Then he snapped his fingers. "And there is some other news. We may receive a visit from a European. They say there is some woman traveling in the country now. She's staying in Kapa and drives out every day to visit the *marabouts* between here and there, coming further south each day. Apparently she visited *Cherno* Bah a few days ago and we might see her even tomorrow."

"Mariama will be excited," said the Hajiya. "She thinks these European women know everything. She'll be happy.

She'll put on her big shoes and wait for the European woman to ask her to go away to London or New York." The Hajiya shook her head. "Yes, Mariama will be happy."

"And not you?" he teased. "I know you'll wear your big earrings, yes?"

"Of course! But these Europeans, they give us nothing but sore ears. They like to come in their big cars and tell us what to do. They tell us they want to work with us but when it comes to money, they give it all to government and government chops it. They are rude and foolish. They want to do good things but they don't even know what a good thing is."

"You are very strong, my dear," said the Alhaji.

"I know what I have seen."

"This Modou of yours," he said, glancing at her with raised eyebrows, "you know that he can speak and understand English?"

"You're very playful tonight," said the Hajiya.

The Alhaji ignored this and continued, "I'll ask him to stay close to the compound. When he sees this European woman arrive, he can stand beside me. They say she has one Fula man with her to translate what is said. She'll talk to him of what she's thinking but I know he'll only tell us what he wants us to hear. They won't think that Modou understands, so he can be my English ears."

From: *The West African Intelligencer*
A weekly news magazine published in London, UK.

Rains Fail in Dazania
By Rick Barry

Poor harvests are the result of low rainfall in the hinterland of Dazania this year. Relief officials estimate that in the northern half of the country household food stocks will provide only 50% of the nutrients required for a proper diet.

The Dazanian government is seeking international aid to avert widespread famine and malnutrition. International agencies have been slow to respond because of the scandal that arose during the last Dazanian crisis, when donated food supplies were shown to have been routed from supply ships directly into the markets, where they were sold to benefit profiteers within the government.

From: *The Masongala Daily Banner*
A daily newspaper published in Dazania.

RKC Office Inaugurated

By Jason Andrews

Ibrahim Jatta, the Hon. Minister of the Interior, hailed the opening of the Rights for Kids Coalition (RKC) office as the first step on the road to full implementation of the UN Convention on the Rights of the Child in Dazania. He spoke to guests assembled at the newly opened office to mark the occasion.

Located on Avenue Yusufu Dafo, the new office is headed by RKC Country Program Director, Reba Brecken. In a speech welcoming government officials and heads of other agencies, Ms. Brecken stated, "This government has taken a proactive stance regarding children's rights that should be emulated by other governments in the region."

RKC is in the process of developing action plans to effect change in all areas of children's rights in Dazania. These plans will be implemented in phases, in partnership with government and non-government organizations.

"Initially we will be working to rescue and rehabilitate the children enslaved in so-called 'darras' in the rural areas. Many of these children are being held in unacceptable conditions and RKC intends to spearhead a program to eradicate such practices," said Ms. Brecken. She received warm applause when she informed the gathering that in order to familiarize herself with the children's circumstances, she intended to trek up country "to gain first-hand experience and reach out to oppressed children."

Darras are Islamic schools operated by marabouts. These men, supposedly well versed in the Koran, gather large numbers of young boys on their rural holdings in order to use their labor to develop profitable farms. Parents are promised that the boys will receive Koranic education in exchange for their labor. Boys often spend most of their childhood years separated from their families while living in darras.

Rights for Kids Coalition is an international NGO that works in partnership with governments and local NGOs, said Ms. Brecken, "to promote and protect the rights of children around the world." It manages programs in 26 LDCs (Less Developed Countries) from its New York headquarters.

Two

The Land Rover bounced over the deep ruts, tossing the woman in the rear seat from side to side in a sickening rolling motion. The driver veered across the road to avoid the cracked craters that suggested that this barren Sahel landscape did occasionally experience rain. Reba Brecken was an attractive thirty-five year old woman with long blonde hair that had begun the day tightly coiled in a bun at the back of her head. Loose strands were now glued to her forehead and the sides of her face with a mixture of sweat and dust. Without relinquishing her hold on the convenient handgrip, she leaned back, closed her eyes and tried to relax.

Her entire being seemed concentrated in her solar plexus, where her intestines writhed and twisted in tight knots. What had started in the morning as a vague feeling of discomfort and heaviness had developed during the day into a painful, churning sensation that was rapidly growing in intensity. She was certain it was the food they had eaten the previous evening. The unidentifiable meat had tasted slightly metallic.

The vehicle and its driver had been loaned to her by Children's Rights in Dazania, the non-government organization that the Rights for Kids Coalition had chosen as their

Dazanian partner. Her general assistant and translator for the trek, Sulayman, worked for the same organization. Both he and the driver had proven to be competent and helpful, but Reba was impatient with them. She found it difficult to understand their lack of empathy. When they encountered children forced to live in dreadful conditions the men remained placid and untouched. The driver and his friendly smile at least had the grace to look hotter and wearier as each day passed. But Sulayman, tall and well dressed, never ceased looking neat and comfortable. He wore the same mildly ironical expression on his face at the end of a grueling day as he did when he greeted her for breakfast. She was thankful that this was the last day of the survey. In a few hours they would return to the guesthouse in Kapa and by tomorrow evening she would be back in her own clean, air-conditioned house in the capital, Masongala.

"Sulayman, how much further is it?"

"Oh Miss Brecken, I thought you were asleep." Sulayman spoke to the driver in the local language, then continued, "He says we will be there in about fifteen minutes."

"When we get there please tell them that I wish to see the sanitary facilities first. I have to use the toilet. Something I ate has affected my stomach and I must relieve myself."

"Ah, your belly is running."

"Whatever. I need to go, badly."

"I will tell them. But Miss?"

"What?"

"This place is not likely to have a proper toilet."

"As long as I can have some privacy, I really don't care at this point. And Sulayman?"

"Yes, Miss?"

"Let's try to make this a very quick visit. I don't want

any hospitality or long discussions. I just want to look at the accommodation and amenities provided for the children, enough to do a rapid appraisal of the situation."

She thought she might just make it through fifteen minutes but a sharp twinge put her on the edge of panic. She seemed to have no control over her lower regions beyond just holding tight and hoping. Something inside her wanted to explode and every bounce of this sadistic vehicle threatened to touch it off. She made a mental note to advise RKC to insist in future that their partners bought vehicles with better springs. This was hell. The nearest Imodium was in her suitcase at the guesthouse several hours' drive distant and there was nothing, nothing at all in this landscape, not a gas station, not a restaurant, not even a house or a hut. A drearily featureless flat plain surrounded her. Stunted shrubs were scattered here and there like wreckage. A swelling of hills smudged the horizon. She unscrewed the cap from her water bottle and took a tiny sip. She was thirsty enough to drink a quart but afraid that it would tip the precarious equilibrium that kept her bowels from releasing their deluge.

"Where we're going, what's the man's name again, please?" she asked. She thought that perhaps if she talked and tried to prepare herself mentally, to put herself into a state of professional readiness, the turmoil in her lower digestive tract might subside.

"Alhaji Bubacar Safo," said Sulayman.

"Alhaji, that means he's been to Mecca. Is that right?"

"Yes, Miss. Sometimes here Alhaji is just used as a name or as an honorary title, but this man is a real Alhaji. He's made the Haj, the pilgrimage to Mecca. And his wife too, she's a Hajiya."

"No disrespect, Sulayman, but why's that such a big deal? Anyone with a few bucks can just go get on a plane. It's not like it's a difficult thing to travel around any more."

"Ah, but the Haj is not just a trip to Mecca to look around and buy a few souvenirs. There are many spiritual exercises you must perform. It's very difficult spiritually, and physically too, to perform the Haj correctly."

"I don't see as it could be any worse than this." She gazed bleakly out the window. "Why do people live up here? Why don't they all just move somewhere decent where there's water and trees?"

"It's their own place. And you're not seeing it at its best, in rainy season. When the rains come it's very beautiful, rich and green, though you won't likely see it then."

"Why not? It sounds like a much better time to do these things."

"You see these big potholes in the road? They're from the rainy season. Most of this area is impossible to get to when the rains come; the roads are just too bad. Often, even, the road is just gone and if you are here you may be stuck in mud for days and stranded in a village for weeks."

The driver interjected a few sentences rapidly in the local language and laughed. Sulayman translated.

"He says to tell you that the mud is very wonderful. Even a big Land Rover like this will just slip and slide and roar until it's up to its headlights in mud. Then you have to find a village that has a donkey to help pull you out. But even once you are free there's nothing to do but get stuck again. And the mud is very sticky, like...."

"OK. OK. I get the picture." She fell silent. The vision of all that mud had broken the momentary calm in her abdomen. Her intestines stretched and tangled themselves with rhythmic contractions of mounting intensity and pressure.

The hills grew more distinct through the windshield and the driver spoke a few words. Sulayman gestured and said, "Beyond those hills is Kafabolo. The Alhaji's compound is on this side of the hills, off to the right."

As Sulayman finished speaking, the driver turned the truck sharply right and it jounced off the road and over an irregular series of bumps until he had slowed to a rocking crawl. "We are nearly there," said Sulayman. "There, you see those houses? That should be the Alhaji's compound." Several mud-brick, thatched huts huddled in the distance. The vehicle bounced across the sculpted furrows of last season's fields.

"Is there no road?" she said through gritted teeth. The question was relayed to the driver and Sulayman translated his answer with a laugh.

"The driver says most of the marabout's visitors come to him on old trails over the hills or from paths that follow the river. He says that if the road had been built for the local people instead of for cars, it would pass very near to the marabout."

Two naked children three or four years old gazed wide-eyed at the Land Rover as it parked outside an opening in the compound's encircling fence. The vehicle ticked as it cooled and settled. A man and woman came out of the largest dwelling. The man was dressed in a light blue flowing robe of the type called a *boubou*. An intricately patterned skullcap covered his head. A checkered red and white shawl was draped over his shoulders and tied loosely across his chest. The woman wore a voluminous dress of brightly patterned cloth with a matching piece of material ornately tied in peaks around her head. Pendulous golden earrings swung from her ears. A skinny young boy in worn shorts followed them and stood beside the man. A few mangy chickens morosely scratched at the hard packed dirt.

"Remember what I said, Sulayman, please, about the toilet."

"Don't worry, Miss," he said as he opened his door. Hot air invaded the vehicle and beads of sweat began itching on her forehead. Sulayman went up to the man, shook his hand and greeted the woman, then indicated Miss Brecken, now exiting from the rear door. He was still speaking to the pair when she came up to them.

The woman turned and shouted into the house. A young teenage girl appeared wearing black, wrap-around sunglasses and a lacy pink blouse. The wrapper she wore below the blouse was colorfully printed with purple cowries on a green background. She hobbled out of the house on yellow plastic platform shoes and shyly smiled.

"This is their daughter, Mariama," said Sulayman. "She will take you to where you can ease yourself."

Miss Brecken flashed what she hoped was a cool and efficient smile at the Alhaji and his wife, then followed Mariama as she made tiny limping steps along a path between the huts. Then they were in the fields, dawdling toward some tufts of undergrowth at the base of the hills. No toilet of any sort was visible and the pressure was mounting. Then it happened. A tiny squirt forced itself out and Miss Brecken knew she had no more than a minute or two before she fouled herself in the most disgusting way. They reached a bushy area and the girl stopped, teetering uncertainly, and held out a jug of water.

"Oh my God," said Miss Brecken. "This is it. No toilet." She dived toward the nearest bush and tore her pants down as she squatted. A violent convulsion jetted the contents of her bowels noisily onto the earth and left her panting and moaning. She saw a brown hand discreetly place the jug of water at her side. Several fat black flies, hairy and iridescent, buzzed excitedly around her, bumping into her as if drunk. One flew up her nostril and she batted at it in panic, lost her balance and toppled backwards into the mess she had made. Another convulsion was building in her and she barely regained her squatting position before she exploded again and was left gasping and weeping. She attempted to console herself. At least she had a roll of toilet paper and some fresh underwear in her handbag. No sooner did this thought arise than she realized that she had left her bag in the truck. This brought on a fresh burst of weeping and another shuddering discharge.

Using the water in the jug she managed to clean much of the mess. Her bowels still grumbled angrily but the worst seemed to have passed. When she looked around, Mariama was standing about fifty meters away, apparently engrossed in the view of the scrub-covered hills. Miss Brecken called the girl over and held out the empty jug. Then she mimed her handbag. Mariama now seemed to understand the urgency. She hiked up her wrapper, slipped off her garish footwear and ran barefoot lightly over the fields. When she returned she was balancing a pail of water on her head and carrying a bar of soap, a towel and the handbag. Twenty minutes later, Miss Brecken followed her back to the compound. She felt light, almost giddy, as she joined the others where they sat on mats in the shade of an overhanging thatch.

The Hajiya's heavy earrings clinked softly as she leaned over and placed a plastic mug of water in front of Miss Brecken. She smiled and pulled her bottle of mineral water from her bag. Sulayman explained she could not drink the local water. Then he translated for her while the Alhaji expressed his great joy at her visit and apologized for being unable to offer her anything more suitable to drink, for the poorness of his hospitality and for the dreadful condition of the countryside. Two boys ran past laughing and chasing one of the lean chickens she had earlier noticed pecking in the dust.

"Fine, fine," she said. "Sulayman, say whatever is appropriate and then let's move along to business. I just want to look around and then leave. I'm not well." Loud squawking and bloodcurdling shrieks came from behind one of the houses, followed by a telling silence.

"He says we must stay to eat. They are killing a chicken in your honor."

"No, no! Please let's just get this over with. Tell him we'll come back and have a nice visit some other time, when I'm feeling better."

Sulayman spoke at length and the pair opposite nodded sympathetically from time to time. Behind the Alhaji the boy sat quietly. Then the Hajiya began to speak and went on and on as if she were elaborating a complex thesis.

"She says," said Sulayman, "that it's impossible that you could come all the way from Europe to see them and they fail to feed you and pay you proper respect. She begs us to stay and eat with them. For them, a visit from someone like you is a very wonderful event. Few Europeans ever come to this compound. She says she knows that what they have to offer is very poor, but you would do them great honor by sharing it."

"Oh Sulayman, they all say that. And I'm not European, I'm American. Please, I want to find out about the children." She busied herself with her clipboard and pen and entered on the forms she carried information she already knew. Sulayman seemed eventually to appease the couple's relentless hospitality and began to feed her the answers she needed for the indentured child labor survey she was compiling. The Alhaji apparently had nine indentured children, all boys, confined here to work as farm laborers. They were unpaid and he expected to retain them for several years at least. She was already convinced that the children here should be re-established with their own families.

"Where are they?" she asked and was told that except for the one who sat with them and the two busy with the chicken, the boys were not in the compound. Some were herding goats and the rest were collecting firewood in the bush. They would return in perhaps an hour or two. If she wished, they could visit the boys with the goats by the river. The Alhaji waved his hand toward the hills and Sulayman explained that the river was about a half hour's walk.

"Very convenient. I suppose he's got most of them out of the way so I can't see them. That one there is probably the healthiest of the bunch and look at him—skinny as a rail! Tell him I want to see where the children sleep and to examine the kitchen."

A few minutes later she stood in what had been described to her as the boys' house, a thatched hut with mud walls that had been plastered inside with some grayish substance a long time before. It was blackened and grubby with innumerable handprints and dirt. It smelled of stale smoke and soot coated the underside of the thatch. There was no furniture. Woven grass sleeping mats were rolled up against one wall. Nearby leaned a stack of wooden slates covered with Arabic writing and by the door was a large clay water pot lidded with a dusty saucer. She made her notes.

"Sulayman, ask the Alhaji to excuse us while we just walk around outside the compound a little so that I can see it properly. And ask this boy to come with us so I can talk to him privately."

As they strolled she said, "I still want to see the kitchen although it's hardly necessary. It's clear this man should not have any children in his care." The sun beat down on her head. She wiped the sweat from her brow with a tissue then fished a hat from her bag. "What is this boy's name?"

Sulayman translated her question and the boy replied, "Modou."

She stopped and knelt, then grasped both of the boy's hands and looked up into his face. "Modou, my name is Reba."

"Reba," he repeated solemnly.

She stood up again. He was really quite a nice-looking boy if only he did not wear such a suspicious expression. He was so thin that she ached to take him away and stuff him full of good food.

"Ask him how he is treated." Sulayman relayed this query to the boy.

"He says he is treated well, that the Alhaji is a good man."

"He's probably been made to memorize all the correct answers," said Reba. "Ask him about the hours they work. From when to when and how many days every week."

The boy answered in an inert voice, speaking slowly.

"He says they work from sunrise until the afternoon. Later in the day the Alhaji gives them some lessons. They work every day but break early on Friday to observe the Sabbath."

"What work is he made to do?"

"Usually, he says, he goes with other boys to take care of the goats. In farming season they do other work as well."

"What do they do with the goats, what is the work involved?"

"They must take the goats to the river so they can drink and try to find places where there is something for them to eat."

The boy here added something in a more animated voice, repeating the word "*mbarodi*" several times. He mimed throwing something.

"What's *mbarodi*?"

Sulayman laughed. "Hyenas. They must also protect the goats from hyenas that try to attack them. He says that earlier in the year there was one big hyena sneaking around in the bush and the boys had to throw stones at it to scare it away."

"Don't hyenas also attack children?"

"Yes, but generally only a very small child. Bigger boys like this one can usually chase them away unless they are taken by surprise."

"But the hyena could have attacked the boys instead of the goats?" persisted Reba.

"Yes. Sometimes when they are many and they are hungry they will attack even a fully-grown person. And even one hyena can kill a big animal like a cow. But normally they are very cowardly."

"Was he afraid?"

"He says no, Miss." Sulayman laughed. "He says I should tell you that if you ever see a hyena you must not be afraid because that is when it will attack you, when you are crying and running away. What you must do is shout bad things at it and run toward it, and throw stones. Then it will run away from you."

"Thank you Modou," she said.

Modou added some more information about *mbarodi*.

"He says you shouldn't run at it too fast. If you get too close it may attack you. Just run at it a little bit."

"Goodness! He seems to have a lot of experience with hyenas."

"These boys must learn how to take care of themselves, even when they are young."

"Sulayman, you mentioned they have lessons. What kind of lessons?"

"He says the Alhaji is teaching them the Koran, that he's a very good teacher."

"Yes, but any arithmetic or history or geography or anything like that?"

"No, only Koranic learning."

She put one hand on the boy's shoulder. It seemed hot and alive. "Sulayman, tell him I want to help him and I want him to help me by telling the truth." She waited while Sulayman translated. The boy looked at the ground, then jerked out an angry sentence.

"He says he always speaks the truth. I think he's a little bit insulted."

"Oh! Please tell him I'm sorry. I didn't mean to insult him," she said and waited for the translation. Then she spoke directly to the boy.

"Modou, don't you miss your family? Wouldn't you like to go back and live with your mother and father again?" She moved her hand from the boy's shoulder up to the nape of his neck and drew him closer while Sulayman translated.

The boy twisted from under her hand and turned away from them. She felt Sulayman was speaking to him too roughly, but he always spoke to children as if they were some form of lower animal. She peered around at the boy's face. He stared stonily into the distance and then two large tears rolled down his cheeks, leaving dark tracks. Sulayman barked at him but he set his jaw and would not answer. Miss Brecken patted Modou on the shoulder, wrapped her arm around him and turned them back toward the compound.

"OK," she said firmly, to put a stop to Sulayman's badgering. "He's given me all the answer I need," she added and was unable to keep her voice from quivering with righteous indignation.

The kitchen was much as she had expected. There was no kitchen at all to speak of, just a large wooden mortar and pestle and a collection of sooty pots jumbled around a stone fireplace. Three or four big enameled basins were piled on a bench near the fireplace and the topmost of these held a worn carving knife and a couple of aluminum ladles. In the adjacent food storage hut were sacks of millet, a large pile of millet still on the stalk, a nearly empty sack of rice and a greasy, half-empty gallon jug of some kind of oil. Several dried fish hung from strings tied to the poles that supported the thatched roof. Other strings held dusty bunches of dried leaves. A few of the large black flies buzzed lazily around the dried fish but seemed to find them too unattractive to invite closer inspection.

"Really, Sulayman," she said once they had regained the

road and the Land Rover's air-conditioning was beginning to make itself felt, "I don't know how those people can live with themselves, keeping children in servitude like that and forcing them to live in such squalor."

"They are very poor themselves and all the children are treated the same as their own. They do the best they can."

"Poor? They struck me as being very well dressed for poor people."

"They probably heard you were coming and dressed like that to honor you."

"Did you see that woman's earrings? I know gold when I see it and those earrings were gold, real gold."

"Ah, those. Those earrings are traditional among the women from around here. She probably got them from her mother. They are only worn on very special occasions. They may be worth a lot but they would never be sold except during a famine or other disaster. They are far more precious than money."

"Perhaps, but I can't get that little boy's face out of my mind. That he should live in such misery instead of living with his own family is simply criminal."

From: *The Masongala Daily Banner*

Darra Children to be Rescued
By Jason Andrews

Reba Brecken, Rights for Kids Coalition Country Program Director, today announced a joint program with the National Police Force of Dazania to rescue children from darras and restore them to their parents. RKC will be subsidizing the NPFD so they can develop special tactical squads that will extract the children from the locations where they are being held and relocate them. Funding of $75,000 will be provided by RKC. The NPFD has committed material and human resources to the program, which is expected to last three months.

Ms. Brecken also announced that in partnership with the Ministry of Information, RKC will be developing a program of nationwide awareness-raising on the issues of child labor, especially as related to the darras. Parents will be encouraged "to care for their children properly at home and to send them to state supported schools." RKC funding of $50,000 has been allocated for the development of appropriate educational materials by the ministry and for the purchase of radio and television advertising over the next year. "Parents need to understand," said Ms. Brecken, "that children should not be considered as sources of cheap labor. They have the right to be educated. They also have the right to play and they need the freedom to do so in order to fully realize their potential as human beings."

NPFD and Ministry of Information officials warmly welcomed the programs as means of developing their capacity to further the rights of children in Dazania.

Three

Nearly a month after the Rights for Kids Coalition's assessment visit, the Alhaji attended the big weekly market in Kafabalo to purchase some cooking oil and hear the news. He sat in the shop of his friend, Gibril, while his host prepared the strong, sweet tea called *attaya*.

"You've heard what happened to Sheik Omar?" asked Gibril, referring to a *marabout* they both knew. He fanned the coals in the small charcoal stove.

"No, is he not well?" asked the Alhaji.

"He has a broken arm, but that's not the worst. The police raided his compound and took all his *talibés* away in a truck. Sheik Omar tried to stop them and they knocked him down. That was when his arm was broken."

"Aiee! This is terrible. What are these police doing?"

"Some European woman visited him, something to do with children. I don't know what. Apparently she was working with the police. Other places she visited, the police are pouncing there also." Gibril poured the tea into a large mug, then back into the enameled teapot to make it stronger.

"What have they done with the children?" asked the Alhaji.

"No-one knows. They were seen driving north but Sheik Omar has not been able to discover much. The police warned him to do nothing and not to talk to anyone or they would put him in jail. One policeman said they were returning the children to their parents. Some have been found wandering near their villages but many are still missing." He handed the Alhaji a shot glass of the powerful tea.

"But what was the reason? They must be having some reason."

"It has something to do with this European woman. At one place the police inspector in charge said they were taking the children because she had reported the marabout was holding them against their will, treating them badly and forcing them to do difficult and dangerous work."

"One European woman came to visit me also..." said the Alhaji.

"In a big Land Rover? One Fula man with her named Sulayman?" queried Gibril.

"Yes. She was ill and didn't like our compound. This is very terrible. I don't understand. Inspector Bah is a good man..."

"It's not our local policemen. Sheik Omar went to Inspector Bah but he said he could do nothing. These men are a special detachment from Masongala, acting under the Inspector General's direct orders. Inspector Bah said they even ordered him to have his men watch the taxi-parks here in Kafabalo to prevent any movement of groups of children."

The Alhaji and his students fled that night. The boys hiked through the hills until they came to the highway on the other side of Kafabalo. There they met the *marabout* who had hired a minivan that would carry them to

Masongala. The boys were excited to travel secretly like this, to evade the police, and they talked through the night. Some had been to the city before with the Alhaji and said that it was good. There were many things to see and different kinds of food to eat.

In the early morning they pulled into a large compound on the outskirts of Masongala. The owner of the compound warmly greeted the Alhaji. He respected the *marabout's* learning and was happy to be able to rent accommodation to him and his students. The owner lived with his family in a large house at one end of a square courtyard. Rooms that opened out into the compound yard formed the other three sides. Relatives of the owner occupied several of these.

The Alhaji rented a small room for himself and an adjacent room for the boys. In the afternoon the Alhaji gave them their lesson in the deep shade of a large mango tree in the center of the compound. The children of the compound sat with them to learn.

When the Alhaji had finished teaching, he said, "I want to speak to you now about our life here. We are guests in this compound and you must all be helpful and respectful at all times. If you see people working you should try to help them. If someone asks you to do something, it's the same as if I were to ask. You will help to keep the compound clean and treat everyone here as if they were your father or mother. Do you understand?"

All the boys nodded and the Alhaji continued, "Tomorrow you will go out into the city to beg. Some of you have done this before and you will teach the others how it is to be done. Sometimes boys feel badly about begging. You must understand it correctly. You know it is one of the pillars of our faith to give charity. When you are begging you are giving other people the opportunity to exercise their charity, to do a good thing. If they keep their money, it will not buy them a place in paradise, but if they give some to you in charity, they may see the doors of paradise open when they die. As *talibés* you are Allah's own children. He has special angels to guard you and He has placed you here to do this service so that others may benefit. When you beg, you will beg in the name of Allah and when you receive alms, you will thank the giver in the name of Allah. Idi will teach you the correct prayers to offer.

"Sometimes people will insult you or treat you roughly when you beg from them. Pay no attention. They are on the road to hell and deserve our pity. Pray also for them. And sometimes other children will make fun of you. They will say you are just ragged beggars. Pay no attention to them either. They are only children and learn such ignorant behavior from their parents. Do not fight with them or return their insults with your own. Just go on your way peacefully. Do you understand?"

The boys nodded.

"In the city, it's not like in the village, where everyone knows everyone else so that wickedness cannot be hidden. Here there are many people, too many to know one by one, and there are bad people who will try to get you to join them in wickedness. Perhaps they will offer you alcohol or some drug. These are very bad things that will spoil your body and your mind. Others may encourage you to be stealing. Run away from such people if you meet them. Do you understand?"

When the boys nodded he added, "Tomorrow when you go into the streets, remember what I have said.

Tonight, our host is giving us a feast to honor our coming. See if you can find some way to be helpful in the preparations."

That night they ate *domoda*, the rich stew made from groundnut paste and palm oil with many big pieces of beef in it. It was served with rice. Every boy was given five pieces of meat on his plate. As was their habit, the boys put their portions of meat to one side of their plates to eat when all else was finished. Modou had never before eaten so much meat. All the boys went to sleep with tight bellies and the conviction that Masongala was a wonderful place to be.

Modou found life in the city interesting. So many people were moving around and every day was different. In the morning the boys divided into three groups since, as Idi said, "Nobody has enough to give to nine boys so we get nothing. But three small boys together do not frighten people." First they visited compounds where they might be given something to eat for breakfast. Storekeepers sometimes gave them a little bread to chew. After a few weeks Modou and the boys he begged with knew certain compounds where the people were kind and if they had more than they needed for breakfast, they would share it with the *talibés*. They called at these compounds on their way toward the big Manjako Market.

In the market, each went his own way, looking for something to do. Perhaps a vendor struggling with a heavy load could be helped. A storekeeper might need to have his store swept. Sometimes the women selling vegetables accepted help in preparing produce for sale, washing carrots or tying bunches of greens together. Fish vendors might let them scrape scales from the fish or fetch ice. For these little services they were paid, maybe a few carrots or tomatoes, an onion or a small fish. When the boys met in mid-morning, they pooled the items they had earned, arranged them neatly on a piece of sacking and sold them cheaply to shoppers looking for bargains.

What Alhaji Safo had said to them when they first arrived had frightened Modou a little but when he had been in the streets for a few days he lost his fear. Generally, people were kind to the *talibés* and were as generous as their purses and hearts permitted. Sometimes the boys were given a few small coins or a handful of rice. Here and there it all added up. Alhaji Safo said he wanted them to try to bring five kuromas to him every day and ten kuromas on Fridays. If they collected more than that they could spend it how they liked or save it to buy themselves new clothing. On Fridays they waited outside the mosque. After prayers, after being reminded of the necessity for giving alms, many people leaving the mosque dropped some change into their pots.

At the compounds where the *talibés* visited regularly and were known, they were included whenever there was a celebration – a naming ceremony, a wedding or the feasts of *Eid ul-Adha* and *Eid al-Fitr*. Sometimes the occasion was sad. One day Modou and two other boys came to the entrance to a compound and were invited inside. There a grieving woman gave them some nearly new boy's clothing. She held up one t-shirt to measure against Modou, then collapsed to her knees, sobbing. Modou put his hand on her shoulder.

"Aieee," she cried. "Oh, my son is gone. My own boy is gone. How can I live like this?" She looked up at Modou and saw a tear rolling down his cheek. "Oh, boy, please don't cry," she said and pulled him to her and held him. "Oh, please don't cry. It will be alright." She rocked him then, stroking his head and crooning. When her sorrow abated she held Modou at arm's length and looked at him steadily.

"What's your name?"

"Modou."

"Modou. Please will you come and visit me every day?"

Every day from that time on Modou and his companions were given breakfast at that compound.

In time, Modou grew to know the market as if it were his own village. Every street and alley, every passageway between the stalls, every vendor and his wares, all were mapped out in his mind. This knowledge earned him a reputation and some extra money. One day a vendor in the inner market asked him to deliver a message to another stallholder near the gates. Modou put down his begging pot and ran as fast as he could, following devious pathways over and around and through the stalls. When he returned, panting, with the response in only a few minutes, the vendor was amazed. "Wonderful!" he exclaimed when he received the answer to his message. "Boy, you are too fast!"

"Too fast" or "Toofas" thus became his name in the market. Vendors knew that if they wanted a message or some small thing delivered quickly, Toofas could get through the market more speedily than any other. Modou loved to do this. It delighted him to run like the wind and twist and turn at top speed through the maze of alleyways and between the shoppers.

One day, a high school student called all the boys in Modou's group to come and talk to a European man. The white man talked through the student because he could not talk any of the local languages. He said he wanted to ask them some questions and he would pay them for their time.

He told them he worked for an organization that wanted to help all the children in the street but before they could make their plans, they had to have more information. Then he asked them all about how old they were and where they came from, how they made their money in the market and how people treated them. He wanted to know whether they worked or begged and where they slept at night. When they had answered all his questions he paid each of them five kuromas and promised he would come back soon to help them. They were happy to earn five kuromas so easily but they never saw the man again.

Another day they were begging for food when a youth invited them to come and eat at a place he knew. They followed him and came to a compound with a big cross over the gate. Inside the compound they could smell the food cooking in the kitchen and the youth said they should just sit down and wait. After they had waited a little a man all in black came out of the house and spoke to them about God. He said he wanted to tell them about a man called Jesus who loved all children and wanted to love them. They were very hungry so they waited patiently while the man talked. Then Idi whispered they should leave because these people were Christians, people who ate pig and drank alcohol. It was not safe to eat their food so they must run. They waited until the man finished speaking and went back into the house. Then they ran out the gate and back to the market as though they were being chased.

As the year turned and the dry and dusty *harmattan* season passed, food stocks in the interior of the country dwindled. The hungry season had begun. The number of *talibés* in the city increased and it became harder for the boys to earn or beg what they needed. Despite their best efforts, some afternoons the boys returned to the compound hungry and far short of the five kuromas the Alhaji had asked them to bring. Then he would take them to a nearby food seller and buy something for their stomachs. This and the fact that it was nearly time to prepare the fields for planting led the Alhaji's mind toward returning to his compound near Kafabalo.

At first, when he heard the Alhaji's plans, the thoughts of traveling in a van again and of seeing the Hajiya excited Modou. But he knew he would miss the busy life of the city. It had carried him a long way away from a past he preferred not to remember. In the city he was seldom reminded of his lost home and family. In the city he was Toofas, the fastest boy in the market.

From: *The West African Intelligencer*

Pickpockets in Paradise?
By Rick Barry

As the economy worsens in the small African nation of Dazania, scores of street children are appearing in the nation's capital city Masongala. Ragged and starving, their hands held out for alms, the children hang out in markets and on the streets and spend their nights huddling in the alleys or taxi-parks of the town. Many of those little hands have now begun to help themselves— to tourist wallets.

Visitors to Dazania should keep tight hold of their purses and wallets when visiting Masongala. This warning was contained in the regularly issued travel advisory from the British Embassy in Dazania. The advisory notes the greatly increased number of street children flocking to the capital in recent months as the primary source of the risk to tourists. "We have numerous reports from tourists who have been robbed recently," said an official of the embassy.

Dazanian Minister of Social Welfare, attending an infant mortality conference in Singapore, could not be reached for comment on this situation but officials in the Ministry denied there was any problem with street children in the city. A Department of Tourism spokesperson referred to the reports as, "highly exaggerated" and stated that tourists were not at risk anywhere in Dazania.

It is estimated that there are as many as 2,000 desperate children in Masongala alone. Such a phenomenon generally indicates deep-seated economic problems and these are widely attributed to the policies of the increasingly despotic rule of President Yusufu Dafo.

From: *The Masongala Daily Banner*

NPFD to 'Relocate' Beggars
By Jason Andrews

Inspector-General of the National Police Force of Dazania today announced the commencement of a joint emergency relocation program in partnership with the Rights for Kids Coalition. "The increasing numbers of street beggars in the city demands action to stem the flow and relieve their deplorable conditions," he said.

The Inspector-General stated that many of the children were not Dazanian but were illegal immigrants from neighboring countries. Children found begging are to be relocated to their home villages or countries of origin. "We are pleased that RKC has responded to this emergency and plan to implement the program immediately," he said.

Tactical squads trained during the Darra Children's Rescue program are to be re-deployed in this program. RKC Country Director, Reba Brecken, said it was a good example of how the "capacity of local agencies is being developed by RKC."

Four

Police Inspector-General Mballo's plan was simple: Two concentric rings, the inner one around the market and its adjacent streets and alleys, and an outer ring around the whole city center to scoop up any of the street children who escaped the market sweep. While police officers blocked all exits from the market, others would comb the interior gathering up beggar children and loading them into waiting trucks. As soon as a truck was filled it would leave for the north. The children would be deposited near their villages and strongly discouraged from returning to the city. The inner ring would move into place at eight in the morning. By this time most of the children would be in the market. The outer ring would then move into position and the roundup would begin.

At dawn, the Inspector-General spoke to his subordinates. "This roundup must be one hundred percent successful. Better you should arrest a few innocent children than that any street children should escape. Some of the market vendors may attempt to hide the children. This constitutes aiding and abetting criminals and should be punished with the utmost severity."

This would encourage the police officers since it was

equivalent to giving them license to plunder the market with impunity at the same time as they arrested the children. The Inspectors and Sub-Inspectors nodded their agreement.

By eleven-thirty in the morning the Inspector-General was back in his office, exhausted but pleased with himself. The last of the trucks had left for the north and most of the officers called in for special duty had been released. Everything was back to normal, except there was not a *talibé* to be seen anywhere in Masongala.

Alhaji Safo worried when his boys did not appear in the afternoon for their lesson. He waited for a few hours then went out to see if he could discover what had happened. Occasionally in past years his boys had been picked up and held in jail. He had always been able to discuss the situation with the police and have the boys released, although sometimes he had had to pay a small fine. Both he and the police simply viewed this as a form of taxation and there were no hard feelings. This day, however, his concern deepened after he met another marabout coming out of the police station and inquired about the situation.

"Aieee! It is too dreadful. They have taken all the children far away from the city," his friend exclaimed and rushed away.

Alhaji Safo entered the police station and spoke to the officer on duty. No, he was told, none of the children were in the jail. All street beggars had been removed from the city by order of the Inspector-General. When he protested, the officer rudely told him that he should not have brought the children to the city in the first place. He should go back to his village and be thankful he was not in jail himself. The Alhaji walked down to the market and spoke to vendors until he located one who had seen some of his boys taken by the police. Then he returned to the compound to think of what he could do.

There he found his brother-in-law awaiting his arrival with a sober face. The Alhaji greeted him and unburdened himself of his worries.

"This is very bad, Alhaji," said the brother-in-law. "But there is worse. I bring bad news."

"Aieee. What could be worse?"

"Be strong, my brother. We are in mourning. The Hajiya, your wife, has died, very early this morning. You must return with me to Kafabalo so we can see to the burial."

The brother-in-law told the story sadly. After Alhaji Safo's hurried departure for the city, the special police had swooped down on his compound at Kafabalo. Incensed at having lost their prey, they spoke roughly to the Hajiya and she had replied in kind. One of the officers became enraged and struck her repeatedly with his baton. During the months that followed she appeared to recover from the beating but her strength was gone. In her weakness she took fever, lingered for some weeks and then died.

The Alhaji listened with his eyes closed. His hands shook as he thumbed his prayer beads. Moisture glistened in the corners of his eyes. In the silence that fell when his brother-in-law finished speaking, the ringing call of the muezzin pierced the Alhaji's grief. From high in the Masongala Central Mosque, the plaintive song summoned the faithful of the city to prayer.

"Allahu Akbar," proclaimed the muezzin sonorously four times. "God is Great." The Alhaji repeated each in a low voice and then gave himself to the rest of the *adhan*, the call to prayer. When it was finished he unrolled his prayer mat and carefully oriented it to face Mecca. "Brother," he said, "It is time to pray." Tears fell onto his prayer mat as he knelt towards the holy city.

⁂

Modou shivered. It had been warmer earlier in the journey. He pulled his t-shirt over his legs for warmth and hugged his knees tightly but the cold wind blew through the worn cotton as if it were not there. The police truck had carried twenty-five boys away from the coast into the colder, drier interior. When they had left the city, the boys had huddled together in the vehicle's open back to share their body heat.

Since darkness had fallen the truck had several times driven off the highway to approach small villages. Boys were roughly ejected from the truck then and beaten before the truck resumed its roaring, bouncing journey through the black countryside. Only four boys remained crouching in the truck. Overhead, the stars glittered. The sky was still so black that Modou knew dawn was many hours away. He hugged himself into a ball and dozed. The truck geared down, indicating they were approaching another stop. They left the highway and jounced slowly over the rutted bumpy road until the light of a few lanterns could be seen glimmering feebly in the distance. The truck came to a halt.

"Jamata," said the policeman, naming the nearby village. The last three boys shook hands with Modou and were pulled over the tailgate into the night. He heard the thud of the nightsticks against flesh and the yelping of the boys as they fled

"Only that one from Selongwe left now," the policeman said as he got into the cab. Modou heard the driver's voice moaning that it was too far. The rest of his complaint was lost when the engine started. The truck whined and growled back toward the highway but when it reached the junction it stopped and the policeman came around and told him to get out. They stood together as the truck reversed and turned.

"We don't want to see you in Masongala again," said the policeman. He lit a cigarette, cupping it in his hand to protect the flame from the chilly wind. "The president doesn't want you in the city and we don't want you. If you come back we'll chase you out again. Go back to your parents." He pointed into the night. "Selongwe is that way." Modou glanced in the direction the policeman indicated. The policeman's nightstick crashed into the side of his head and he fell to the ground. The officer got into the cab and the truck headed back toward Masongala.

When Modou regained consciousness the bitter cold had seeped inside his bones. He feared to touch the side of his head. By the light of the moon he saw a jumble of rocks near the roadside that might offer some shelter from the wind until morning. He stumbled toward them and felt his way into a cleft between two large boulders. He was shaken by bouts of shivering so intense it seemed he must break into pieces. Then suddenly his body would be still and he ached all over. He tried to warm his hands beneath his armpits, then chafed his legs and feet. He drifted in and out of sleep. The wind died as the sky grayed into dawn.

He walked beside the road in the opposite direction to that given by the policeman. He had no wish or reason to return to Selongwe. The sun came up and its welcome warmth spread through his body. The sun climbed higher in the sky and he began to feel thirsty. When the sun was overhead he saw the thatched roofs of a small compound not too far distant from the highway. There he could find water and perhaps, some food. As he drew nearer, however, his hopes began to fade. No sound came from the compound and the roofs had fallen in on several of the houses. He entered the compound yard and called a greeting. There was no answer.

Behind the houses he found a well and beside it was a worn plastic jug, still attached to a rope. Once he had drunk his fill he felt less desolate and looked around more closely. He should check the houses in case someone had left some food or something else he could use. The compound was crumbling back into the earth but he could see that it had been occupied until recently. A three stone fireplace had ashes in it that looked almost fresh and an overturned pot lay nearby. He found a mortar and pestle in the hut nearest the fireplace. There was a handful of powdery pounded *coos* in the bottom of the mortar. He stuffed it into his mouth and chewed it slowly until he could swallow it. On the floor beside one wall of the hut was a piece of sacking where some heads of coos were piled. He sat down and rolled these between his palms to free the tiny, rock hard seeds. He would fill his belly before he continued his journey. First the seeds must be pounded to remove the outer husk. He moved the mortar and pestle into the compound yard and began to pound the grains. Pum! Pum! Pum! Then he heard a low cry. He stopped pounding the *coos* and listened intently, but the sound was not repeated.

The cry seemed to have come from one of the huts he had not examined. He had seen beside that hut the mounds of two recent graves and had looked quickly away. Now he pulled aside the ragged curtain that hung over the door and peered inside. A body lay on a sleeping mat. It was a boy, smaller than himself, and still alive. He was unconscious and Modou could not wake him. He brought water from the well and raised the boy's head. It rolled drunkenly in his hand. The cracked lips were stuck together. He gently opened them with his finger and let drops fall into the slack mouth until the water began to dribble away. Then he laid the boy down and bathed his face. The body was limp and the bones seemed loose inside it. The boy's skin was hot and dusty and Modou dipped a rag in water and washed his chest and arms. Then he lifted his head again and held the cup to the swollen lips. The boy's eyes opened and looked into Modou's for a few seconds, then closed again. Modou folded a cloth into a pillow and tucked it under the boy's head. Then he went back to pounding the *coos*. He found a matchbox in the cooking hut, fetched some firewood and started a fire. He interrupted his tasks regularly to bathe the boy with cool water and make him drink.

Though he had learned to pray properly from the Alhaji, Modou had never prayed with his whole heart. He had seemed never to want anything so he had had no reason to pray. Now as he prepared food his mind endlessly begged, "Please let him live. Please let him live." By the time the porridge had cooked, the boy appeared to be sleeping peacefully. His body was cooler and when Modou held the cup to his lips he swallowed instead of letting the water spill down his chin. Modou ate until his stomach was full. Then he carried the remaining *coos* into the hut where the boy lay. He lifted him up to give him more water and the boy's eyes opened again. He sat up by himself.

"Salaam Alaikum," said Modou

"Alaikum as-Salaam," replied the boy.

"What's your name?" asked Modou.

"Umaru."

"I'm Modou."

"Modou," said the boy slowly. Then his eyes filled with tears.

Modou reached out and the boy fell against him. "I know," he said, wrapping him in his arms. "I know." When the racking sobs had subsided Modou bathed the boy's face again.

"You must eat," he said and placed the pot of *coos* porridge between them. Darkness fell while the boy ate. The wind rose and moaned between the compound walls. Modou built a small fire inside the hut and fastened the covering over the door. He lay down beside the boy and pulled a cloth over them.

Modou awoke once during the night. Across his chest lay the boy's arm and his breath warmed Modou's shoulder. Something loosened in his heart and he smiled. He tucked the cloth more tightly around them and they slept deeply until the sun was in the sky.

When they woke they were a little shy and Modou rolled away and stood up.

"Aieee! We've slept so late." He picked up the pot and sat down opposite Umaru. "Now let us eat a little." They ate some of the cold rubbery porridge and Modou wrapped the lump that remained in a cloth. "We'll wash ourselves now, and then we must leave."

Umaru trailed him wordlessly to the well, where they drank and washed their hands and faces. "Come," said Modou, leading the way toward the highway. Umaru stood and looked at him, then began to turn to look back. "Don't look, Umaru. It'll be easier if you don't look."

Umaru stopped turning, gazed at Modou for a long moment and then followed him.

Traffic was light. They waved at the few trucks that passed but none stopped. They spoke little. At noon they rested in the shade of a small tree and ate what remained of the *coos*.

"Where are we going?" asked Umaru.

"To the city. Have you been to the city?"

"No."

"It's very nice," said Modou. "There are many people. Most are good but some are not so good. There's a lot of food and a lot of money. We'll find my Alhaji and he'll tell us what to do." Then he told Umaru of the markets and the stores with televisions in the window and the fishermen's beach and the taxi parks and all about the best places to beg.

In the evening they came to a small village. A kind woman gave them a supper of rice with oil on it and let them sleep in her hut.

The following afternoon a truck stopped and the driver invited them to ride in the cab with him for a few kilometers. When he stopped he shared his lunch with them. They walked until evening but no village was in sight when the sun dipped below the horizon so they sought shelter on a rocky hillside near the road. They built a fire and shared the bread the driver had given them. It was a calm night and the moon shone brightly. When they had eaten the bread they curled up beside each other and went to sleep.

Modou woke in the night, suddenly alert, and sat up quietly. He heard again the slight crackling of dry leaves that had warned him of an intruder. He reached over, stirred the coals of the fire and threw a handful of grass on it. In the flickering light he saw something move in the shadows. The bushes rustled. He picked up a stick and moved toward the sound. He climbed a boulder and peered into the darkness. Then he saw the wild boar. He threw the stick and hit it on the nose. It leaped sideways, squealing, then grunted and trotted away on its stiff little legs as if insulted. Modou strained his ears for several minutes and heard only the beating of his own heart. The murderous mad laughter of a pack of hyenas faintly etched the night air. The sound carried a great distance but the pack moved away as he listened.

Umaru was sobbing by the fire but stopped when Modou returned

"Only a wild boar," said Modou.

"I thought you ran away and left me."

"Aieee," said Modou. "You're such a small small boy. How could I leave you?" He threw some thick sticks on the fire to keep it burning brightly through the night, then pulled Umaru down next to him. "I'll never leave you, foolish boy. Now let's sleep. If we start early we may reach the city tomorrow."

They were lucky in the morning and got a ride for an hour with a friendly trucker. He said he had no food with him but gave them some water before he dropped them. The morning stretched into late afternoon before another trucker stopped. He also let them ride in the cab. He whistled and sang while he drove.

"Sir," said Modou, "do you have anything for us to eat? We have not eaten since yesterday and we are very hungry."

"I was looking at you," said the driver, "and I was thinking you looked like about the two hungriest boys I've seen for a long time. Of course, boys are always hungry. But you look especially hungry. So I am sad because I have no food, not one bite, in this my truck. But," he said, "I am also happy because up ahead, you see, just over that little hill, is Safo Town, where my wife is having a small restaurant. Now my wife is a very good cook. But she really only likes to feed people who are very, very starving, so she will be very happy when I am bringing two hungry boys. I like very much to make my wife happy so I am thanking you boys for being hungry. It's very kind of you."

Although their bellies were aching with emptiness, Modou and Umaru had to laugh. "You're a funny man," said Modou.

"Ah, wait 'til you meet my wife. She is much funnier. But I'm sorry, she's probably going to trouble you about your head. It looks like you had an accident, no?"

By the time Modou had explained about the roundup and policeman they had pulled up in front of a small restaurant on the outskirts of Safo Town. Rusty roofing sheets formed three walls and a roof that provided shade for two long tables. It was open to the road in the front. Delicious food smells came from the kitchen in the rear. The man's wife refilled the boys' plates until they had to beg her to stop. Then she washed Modou's head wound and put some ointment on the broken skin.

When she had finished, the man spoke seriously to Modou. "Now, you will please forgive me."

"Sir, you are too good," protested Modou.

"No. I'm a wicked man. You see, I'm longing to spend this night here with my wife, so I won't be going to Masongala until tomorrow. Now I know you're probably in a great rush to be on your way and it's very cruel of me not to carry you there right away."

"It's true, we have very important business in

Masongala," said Modou solemnly, but his eyes were laughing.

"I knew it!" said the man. "But I am going to ask you to do a favor for me, please. You see, in my house behind this place I have one extra bed that is very lonely since no one ever sleeps on it, unless it is my brother coming from Kapa. Would you mind to sleep on that bed with your friend tonight? It will make that bed so happy! My house will be singing! And then, as well, I can have the pleasure of your company on the road tomorrow."

"Well," said Modou, "it is a lot to ask. You know, there are so many beds in the world."

"True! True!" exclaimed the man.

"And you have treated us so badly since we have come."

"It's true I'm sure. But how have I made you suffer?"

"Since we arrived we have been sitting here with dirty hands. This is making us very uncomfortable, you know. I am waiting patiently for your to notice, but you're just a selfish blind person who thinks only of yourself."

The man buried his head in his hands, but Modou continued relentlessly.

"You see our hands are very dirty from traveling, traveling, traveling. If you had a big basin and perhaps some soap and perhaps some dirty pots, I thought you might let us use them. You know, washing pots is the best way to get hands clean. But no, I suspect your wife is keeping all the dirty pots for her own pleasure, without thinking of the needs of passing strangers."

The man looked at his wife, "My dear, he speaks the truth. We are too thoughtless."

His wife let out a cry, "Aieeee, husband, all day I look forward to the evening when I can at last wash my pots and now you bring these two strangers into the house like this. Well, if they insist, how can I refuse? They have already done so much for us by helping us to get rid of all that extra food, a few dirty pots are little enough for us to offer in return."

Modou and Umaru washed the pots and pans and all the dishes and helped the woman in the kitchen until everything was neat and clean and shining. By then it was dark. The man said he was worried because the pressure in the water tank behind his house was too high and asked if they could help him out by going into his bathhouse and draining off some of the water.

When they had finished soaping themselves and letting the cool water run over their bodies, they stepped out of the bathhouse and found their clothes were missing. Two clean wrappers were draped over a branch by the bathhouse door. "I am so sorry," called the woman from her doorway. "I am so clumsy. I was moving around there and your clothes fell into some soapy water, just by accident. I have hung them up to dry. I hope you are not angry with me."

Modou looked at her silhouetted against the lamplight and ran to her and hugged her tightly. "Ma," he said, "You're a very foolish woman."

"I am trying," she said softly and stroked his damp neck.

In bed that night after they had said their goodnights and were giving themselves to sleep, Umaru suddenly turned to face Modou and spoke into his chest. "Your mother, what is her name?"

"Mata," said Modou. "Her name was Mata. In my village they called me Modou-Mata."

"She is dead?"

"All, all are dead."

"My mother's name was Fatou."

"Fatou," said Modou.

They lay quietly for some minutes, then Umaru said, "Modou," as if tasting the sound inside himself.

Modou smelled the clean, soapy scent rising from the boy's head and heard the night birds' cries. "Umaru," he said and they slept.

On the road, stuffed full of breakfast, wearing clean shorts and t-shirt and feeling as new and fresh as the morning, Modou watched the sun rising over the rushing highway with a sense of excitement. They sang and laughed until they reached the outskirts of Masongala. The man said he wished Masongala were further away. He had complained to the authorities but nothing had been done about it so he would just have to accept that their journey together was ended.

Modou directed the driver to the compound where he had been staying with the Alhaji. The truck stopped and the boys got out and walked around to the driver's door. Modou's throat tightened when he reached up and shook the man's hand. Umaru did the same. Then Modou found his voice and truly felt the meaning of the Arabic prayer that had passed his lips a thousand times before.

Thank you

May God accept your gift

May God reward you

May God give you what you want in life

"You're a *talibé*," said the man. "I think you have a good teacher."

"You also are a good teacher," said Modou.

"Go with God, boy," the man said after a moment. "And you," he said sternly to Umaru, "you take care of this

Modou boy. Don't leave his side. He's too foolish to walk around this crazy world alone. You promise?"

Umaru nodded.

They watched the truck until it was lost to sight, then walked toward the compound gates. Inside, the compound yard was empty. Modou called a greeting and a small girl came out of the house and shyly greeted them. He asked to see the Alhaji. The child ran into the house. They looked into the rooms that had been occupied by the Alhaji and his students. They were empty. The boys seated themselves cross-legged on the ground in the shade of the mango tree and waited. In a few minutes the grandmother came out of the house, greeted them and brought cool water for them to drink. Then she sat down and told them of the death of the Hajiya and the departure of the Alhaji and other compound members to attend the funeral. She did not expect the Alhaji to return.

Modou's eyes filled with tears. It seemed that death was following him everywhere as if it were his shadow. He lay on his side in the dust and cried. He cried for the Hajiya. He cried for his family. Umaru patted his back until he too was overcome and crumpled beside Modou as the sobs shook his body. Their sorrow was like a wind that swept through the compound and soon the grandmother's face too was buried in her hands. The child's face then wrinkled in dismay and she rushed to the old woman and wept into her lap. When they were exhausted and peace had returned to them the old woman produced some money from the folds of her clothing. The Alhaji had left it behind, she said, to be given to any boys who came to find him.

Modou accepted the money with thanks. When they left the compound they turned their faces toward the city.

From: *The Masongala Daily Banner*

Dazania Hosting Africa Summit on CIDC
By Jason Andrews

Delegates from sixteen African nations and numerous international NGOs are meeting this week at the prestigious, five star Makalo Beach Hotel to discuss the problems of Children in Difficult Circumstances (CIDC) in Africa.

In her opening speech this morning, Dazania's First Lady, The Honourable Mrs. Safiatou Dafo, welcomed delegates to Dazania and said that the summit would, "address the problems of African children within the context of the UN Convention on the Rights of the Child and facilitate networking between African countries and agencies working with children in Africa."

In the keynote address, Ms. Reba Brecken, Country Representative of the Rights for Kids Coalition (RKC), stated that the summit had been, "designed not only to discuss the common problems faced by African children but to assist delegates to examine specific problems in their own countries and measures taken to address these problems. From this examination we propose to work together in drawing up country-specific action plans that delegates can implement when they return to their own countries."

Ms. Brecken went on to state that the first step in each action plan would be for delegates to call for Task Forces on CIDC to be assembled in their own countries. The purpose of these would be to examine existing legislation in light of the Convention on the Rights of the Child and propose changes in the legislation to bring it into line with the convention. The second purpose of the Task Forces would be to examine research that has been done on CIDC in each country and determine whether it was adequate to provide a basis for planning programs to protect the rights of children. The third "most important" activity of the Task Forces would be to design implementation plans based on existing and new research and legislation.

President Yusufu Dafo hosted a gala banquet for delegates at the Presidential Palace after the first day's meetings. RKC has provided substantial funding for the summit, which will last until next Thursday.

From: *The Masongala Daily Banner*

RKC Approves Research
By Jason Andrews

Rights for Kids Coalition Country Program Director Reba Brecken and Ministry of Social Welfare officials today announced they have agreed on the Terms of Reference for a $50,000 research program on street children.

Ms. Brecken said that the study would provide baseline data that currently impedes program planning for these children. "Previous studies failed to distinguish between children living in the street, children begging in the street, children working in the street and the various permutations such as children working in the street but living at home, children working only part-time in the street, etc." Time-lines and seasonal variations in street child populations will be analyzed. Researchers will also explore drug use, sexual activity and other health issues amongst street children. "The final study will enable program planning to ensure the rights of these children are respected," said Ms. Brecken.

From: *The West African Intelligencer*
A Weekly Newsmagazine published in London

Coup Imminent in Dazania?
By Rick Barry

Increased numbers of heavily armed soldiers in the streets of Dazania's capital city, Masongala, over the last few days have prompted rumours of an imminent coup in this small West African country. Dazanian military sources scoffed at the rumours and said that the soldiers were simply a response to the British Embassy's recent travel advisory warning tourists of pickpockets.

Informed observers, however, suggest that the British Embassy issued the warning to travelers, not because of increased risk of theft but because they wish to deter tourists from visiting Dazania when there is danger of a coup. They are thus able to discourage tourists without seeming to slight the stability of the Dazanian government.

A spokesman for the National Police Force of Dazania has stated that there has not been any increase in the number of thefts. He further stated that tourists have never been at risk and are even less so since the recent street children relocation program was completed with one hundred percent success. Ministry of Tourism officials agreed with the police that the British Embassy's warning had no substance in fact. One can only wonder, in that case, what the soldiers are doing in the streets, except to provide a show of force to would-be coup plotters.

Five

Manjako Market hummed like a beehive in the center of Masongala. Long before they reached its gates, Modou and Umaru jostled through crowds of hawkers and shoppers along sidewalks lined with little stalls displaying tooth-sticks, mango slices, peeled oranges ready for sucking, combs, nail clippers, scissors, and myriad other useful things. The throng's ceaseless movement gravitated toward the market gates and even the stalls seemed to be edging toward the market, carried along on the drift of sellers' cries and the buzz of sales being negotiated. Modou attached Umaru's hand to his t-shirt so he would not be swept away by the waves of pedestrian shoppers. Wide-eyed and excited, Umaru gripped this lifeline tightly.

"Toofas!" called a man as they passed through the market gates. The boys went to greet him by his bar-row full of green African oranges. At the front of the barrow was a high pyramid of curling peels. He cut a small circle in the top of a peeled orange and handed it to Modou, who gave it to Umaru. The vendor grabbed another peeled orange and prepared it for Modou. The boys squeezed and sucked the thirst quenching juice out of the oranges.

"You looking good, Toofas. Only one little smash up for side of head there," said the orange vendor.

"Roundup," said Modou, dropping into the telegraphic market language. "This my friend, Umaru."

"Umaru. You boys go watch plenty. Police still looking around but maybe you OK after two, three days. Don't be begging now now, maybe just be doing small work."

The boys thanked him and moved on into the market. Arranged in ordered rows were the official stalls, large three sided spaces with pull-down metal gates that could be lowered over their open fronts at night. These shops spilled their merchandise into the broad aisles before them. Nearby, in every available space, merchants were tucked into corners with their wares spread out on small portable tables or bits of sacking, so that everywhere were things to buy and people eager to sell them. Many more modest stalls built of pieces of iron roofing sheets, wood and cardboard surrounded these official stalls in a twisting labyrinth, with sellers of similar items such as clothing, shoes, vegetables and fish grouped together.

"What're we going to do here?" asked Umaru.

"We're going to live here," said Modou. "This is our village now."

As they walked toward the rear of the market where the fish market backed onto the beach, Modou was greeted again several times.

"Why does everyone call you 'Toofas?'" asked Umaru.

"It's my market name. They like to call me Toofas because I run fast; in English they say, 'too fast.' Listen, Umaru, it's easy to get lost here. You just stay by me until you know what to do. If you get lost, sit down until I find you. Don't be wandering around. OK?"

Umaru nodded.

"You hungry?"

Umaru nodded again.

They went to a food seller and sat down on the bench in front of her kitchen. Modou greeted the woman and asked for two plates of rice.

"Toofas, you are having money today?" said the woman.

"Small money is there. Today is vacation, just enjoying today."

"Nice for you, vacation. For me is just working, working, working."

"Maybe tomorrow we go come for help you, wash all your dish, sweeping everything, make all nice nice for you. You looking tired. Maybe even now you let us help you small," said Modou grabbing a couple of the local palm fiber brooms. He handed one to Umaru and they began sweeping the floor of the stall, under the benches and tables.

"Two plates of rice is three kuromas, each one," said the woman.

"Is no problem," said Modou, smiling. "We are having money. Is nice you let us sweep. All day we be walking around looking for a good woman who is working hard, who is tired, so we can do a little sweeping. Is not work for us, is play." He laughed and danced a few steps while he swept.

"Three kuromas each plate," said the woman.

"We come all the way through market to find you because you cook the best rice," said Modou. "You are like our Ma – of course we go sweep for you. Is no problem three kuromas for such good rice, even four kuromas each plate is a good price."

The woman laughed from her belly and said, "Oh, Toofas!"

Modou neatly swept together the small piles of dust, rice grains and fish bones he and Umaru had gathered, pushed them onto a piece of paper and deposited it in a nearby trash can. The woman put two mounded plates of rice in front of them. Each had a large piece of fish in the center of the plate.

"Is big fish, Ma," said Modou, licking his fingers when they had finished. "Thank you."

The woman said, "Give me two kuromas each plate."

"You a good woman, Ma," said Modou as he paid her the four kuromas. "Maybe you help us small. We like to be in fish business – what kind fish this?"

"Today is kobo," answered the woman.

"How much you pay for this kobo?" asked Modou.

"Paying two kuromas for three, sometimes four if they small."

"You are buying in fish market every morning?"

"Mmm," nodded the woman.

"Maybe if someone go bring kobo here tomorrow, nice price, you are buying?"

"Maybe."

"Not for money, but maybe for some good cooking, nice plate of rice, maybe?"

"Only fresh kobo, nice ones."

"Best kobo, special ones for you," said Modou.

"Is business now," said the woman.

"Thank you Ma," said Modou. "Maybe we go see you tomorrow morning."

"Toofas," said the woman, "only fresh ones."

"We not going to carry them," said Modou. "They going to run up from beach, ask to jump in your pot."

When they left the food seller, Modou was hailed by

a vendor who wanted him to carry a message to a supplier near the market gates.

Modou pulled Umaru forward. "This my friend. He from the village, don't know anything. Maybe he get lost."

"He go sit here 'til you back," said the vendor.

"You go watch him?" said Modou.

"OK, don't worry. I go watch him. Go now."

Modou sat Umaru down beside the storekeeper and raced toward the gates. Umaru fidgeted and worried. It seemed Modou was gone a long time. But when he returned with the merchandise the vendor had requested, the man was happy with how fast he had run and gave him one kuroma.

Modou pocketed the coin and then took Umaru by the arm. "Have you ever seen the ocean?" he asked.

"What is that? Ocean?"

"You'll see," said Modou.

The beach behind the market consisted of a narrow sandy strip with here and there some straggling mangrove shrubs and patches of mud. It was heavily littered with torn plastic bags and containers. Beyond the market on one end where the water deepened, there were some wooden piers where ships docked. Directly behind the market was a longer stretch of sandy shoreline where the fishermen beached their canoes and sold their catches to the market women. Past the market this sandy strip grew narrower and muddier and the mangroves grew more closely together to form the tidal swamp known as the *bolong*. This muddy, nearly impenetrable bush stretched twenty-five kilometers along the coast from Masongala until it reached the long sand beach known as Makalo, where the tourist hotels were clustered.

Modou and Umaru stood on the edge of the water with the waves lapping their toes. With a grand sweep of his arm Modou pointed west and said, "That way is America." Then he pointed north and said, "and that way is Europe."

"Can you see it?" asked Umaru, squinting into the distance.

Modou laughed, "No, it's too far. Even in a big boat it takes a long time, maybe two or three weeks, to get there."

As they walked back toward the market Modou greeted a street boy he knew. The boy said that he and some other boys had a house further along the beach and Modou and Umaru were welcome to come and stay with them that night.

"You are having food there?" asked Modou.

"Only some bread," said the boy.

"Maybe we go buy one tin sardine," said Modou. "Is how many boys?"

"Is eight, maybe ten," said the boy.

"Maybe two tin sardine," said Modou.

"Is nice," said the boy. "Sardine and bread."

The market boys' house consisted of scraps of plastic tarpaulin and large garbage bags tied over a framework of branches and bicycle frames about three meters across and a meter and a half high. Inside, the floor was covered with worn out rice sacks, pieces of cloth and a couple of old foam mattresses. Boys arrived from the market throughout the evening. Some brought fruit or bread and when all the residents were gathered the food was shared. They applauded Modou's tins of sardines. The boys built a small fire in front of the house and sat around it until late, talking and telling stories. Modou and Umaru were not the only new residents. About half the boys who had lived there had been scooped up while sleeping late during the last roundup and new boys had moved in to replace them. After the other boys had drifted off to sleep, Modou lay awake thinking.

In the morning he woke Umaru early and they walked down the shore to where the fishermen beached the large fishing canoes called *gals*. The canoes were still at sea, barely visible in the gray early morning light. The boys squatted on their haunches on the sand to wait.

"You OK?" asked Modou after a few minutes of silence.

Umaru drew lines in the damp sand between his bare feet and sniffled. Modou could see tears in his eyes when the other boy looked up and out to sea. "I don't know," said Umaru, "not too good, I think."

Modou draped his arm around Umaru's shoulder and pulled him close. Umaru's shoulders quaked and Modou patted him until his crying quieted. "It's OK to be sad," said Modou. "But not all the time. Sometimes you just have to put the sadness away. Then after a while it doesn't hurt so much."

Umaru nodded.

"Now smell this ocean. I like that salt smell, so clean."

Umaru sniffed and smiled weakly. "Yes, it's a good smell. Makes me hungry."

Modou pointed to where the first of the brightly painted *gals* was nearing the shore. "First we will do small work. Then we will eat. That is how we do here."

"It's nice, that house, nice sleeping with so many boys," said Umaru as they trotted towards the canoe.

"Yes, but it's foolish, too," said Modou. "Policemen know that house. Next time there is a roundup they'll just pick up all the boys there."

"They were saying last night no roundup for a long time, not many boys in the market now."

"When the next roundup comes we'll be living somewhere else. Maybe we'll find our own house today, some place the police won't look. Now let's help these fishermen with their canoes."

The boys ran out into the waves, returned the fishermen's shouted greetings and grasped the sides of the canoe to pull it up onto the sand. Because the catch had been good, the fishermen were generous and gave them a few of the small fish called kobo. After the market women had filled their basins with fish, Modou and Umaru helped carry these to the fish market. They were paid a few more small fish for this service and traded their earnings to the food seller woman for the promise of two plates of rice later in the day.

"Lunch is OK, now," said Modou with satisfaction. "Now we'll go have breakfast like rich boys." He led them to a stall where the stallholder prepared plastic mugs of sweet milky coffee for them and made two sandwiches with fried eggs in bread. Modou paid with some of the money the Alhaji had left for him.

"This is good," said Umaru. "Thank you Modou."

"Got to feed you up," said Modou. "Got to train you up too. Today you're going to learn market. There are many ways to go around, some fast, some slow. And there's some small ways only boys can go. When roundup comes you're going to know just how to run and where to hide."

"This market is very big."

"Don't worry. I'm going to teach you everything."

They were never still that day. They walked from one side of the market to the other, and across it from the gates in front to the beach at the rear and back and forth diagonally a dozen different ways. In the late afternoon Modou tested Umaru, asking him to lead them to this or that stall. That night they waited until business had ceased for the day and then lay down to sleep under a counter in the open-air fish market.

"Now I know this market," said Umaru as they settled themselves for sleep.

"Yes, you're learning fine fine. But now you're knowing only one market. All you know is the slow market for people just walking around," said Modou. "Tomorrow I'll teach you another market, fast market, for boys who are running. When we're looking for work we just walk around like normal. But when we want to move fast, we're going to go where nobody is seeing. I'll teach you."

The next day Modou showed Umaru the secret passages behind some of the shops, how some stalls opened into the backs of other stalls, where narrow openings between stores provided short cuts between aisles, how to duck under shop counters and pass through to other aisles, and places where it was possible to climb up onto the roofs of the market and under the foundations of buildings. At the end of two days Modou was satisfied that Umaru could, if it were necessary, escape the market unnoticed. They arranged an emergency rendezvous in the *bolong*, a half kilometer distant from the market. Sometimes during the training, Modou was asked to deliver messages or goods to other parts of the market. He always deposited Umaru safely in the custody of a stallholder before he ran off on these excursions.

At night they continued to sleep in the fish market. They had found a big piece of cloth to cover themselves with, but both were restless in their sleep.

"You're itching," said Modou, scratching his crotch energetically as they settled in for the night.

"You're itching too," said Umaru. He had scratched his hands so much during the day that they were oozing and scabbed between his fingers but the itching was worse and seemed to be spreading to other parts of his body.

"Got some problem," said Modou. "Everything is itching. My penis is itching too much. When he stands up he wants to cry."

"Mine too. Standing up or lying down he's crying. Maybe it'll go away, tomorrow," offered Umaru.

"Insh'Allah," said Modou. "We got to find some money tomorrow. Training is finished now and money from Alhaji is finished too. Tomorrow we'll take a good bath on the beach, with soap, maybe fix this itching problem. It's nice for penis to be itching, but not all the time like this."

Some of the market boys and beggars who had been carried away in the last roundup had returned to the market but the population was still low so it was easy to find work most days. Modou generally ran errands and Umaru began to find little jobs he could be doing while Modou was running around. Now that Umaru was familiar with the market and had learned the escape routes, Modou worried less about leaving him on his own.

One day the fishermen had not been able to catch many fish so the boys went without their lunch. They met another market boy who said they should come with him to a place called "All God's Children," where there was a good man who sometimes gave food to the street boys. When they arrived they were each given a small plate of rice. The man who fed them was named Mr. Cham. He was kind and friendly and said they could come again for food in three days.

"I see you boys are having *wagga*," said Mr. Cham.

"Yes," said Modou, "itching is too bad."

"I am having some cream for that," said Mr. Cham. "In English, the name for *wagga* is scabies. When you finish eating, come into the house and I'll show you what you must do to stop that *wagga*."

In the house he had them take off their clothes. He gave them two towels, a bucket of water and some soap, then led them to a bathing place behind the house and told them to wash well all over. When they came back into the house he gave them a bottle of white lotion and told them to put it all over their skin from the neck down, every place.

"Toofas, you put it on Umaru to make sure cream is on every last place, and Umaru, you're going to put it on Toofas, all over where he can't reach. OK?"

They nodded and he went out to feed some boys who had just arrived.

"Finish?" he inquired when he came back in. They nodded. "OK. Now, here's the problem: *wagga* is a very small thing and he likes to hide inside cloth so you can't be wearing these clothes again." He handed them two used but clean shorts and t-shirts. "Put these on and be listening to what I am saying. Probably you got that *wagga* from sleeping with other boys. The *wagga* is in their clothes or in the sheets on the bed. You must be sleeping somewhere else from now on or you're just going to have *wagga* again. If you got one cloth you're using to sleep at night you should throw it away or not use it again until you wash it well with soap. If you do what I say, this *wagga* will go away in two or three days. You understand?"

"We not sleeping with other boys now now," said Modou. "And we go find one new cloth for our sleeping place."

Within a few days the boys had stopped itching and a week later, after their morning swim, Modou examined Umaru and himself critically.

"Very nice," he said, "look at this penis, it's like new!"

Umaru laughed as he reached for his shorts. "If the market women see you on the beach like that, with your penis standing up and looking around, they'll beat you!"

As the weeks merged into months, the number of *talibés* and market boys increased and it became more difficult to find work or beg food. Some days Modou and Umaru ate only one meal and went to sleep hungry. If they had been apart in the afternoon, the boys always met at sunset by a certain log on the beach, to pool their earnings and share what food they had been able to get.

One evening Modou ran up to Umaru where he waited by their log. "Umaru boy, you got any money?"

"Two kuromas. You?"

"Four kuromas. It's good. Come! We're going to have a nice time tonight."

As Modou dragged Umaru down the beach he explained. "You know Salif, that big boy?"

"Mmm."

"And his sister, that beautiful big girl, Aja?"

"That one sexing the big men for twenty kuromas?"

"Yes. They got one message from their village today. Their mother's sick. She wants them to come home and bring money for medicine now now."

"So?"

"Salif is saying to me they got no money, so anyone who wants to be sexing Aja tonight is going to be paying only three kuromas."

"They'll just laugh at small boys like us."

"Not tonight. Tonight even a dog with three kuromas is going to be sexing. See, that's their fire there!" Modou pulled Umaru into a trot.

"Spending money for sexing, no money for food," said Umaru.

"Food is any time, but tonight, one night only, three kuroma plate special sexing. Don't worry. I'll go first, then you'll be knowing what to do."

Several other boys stood and sat around the fire talking to Salif. Aja lay on her back on a mat nearby.

Modou greeted Salif and the other boys. "Here's six kuromas for two customers," he said and gave the coins to Salif.

"Aja," called Salif. "Take this Toofas boy and Umaru now." Then he said to Modou, "OK, go now, but don't be too long, I see some other boys coming."

Modou and Umaru walked over to where Aja lay. Modou pulled off his shorts and handed them to Umaru. Then he lay down between Aja's legs.

"Toofas boy, it's nice to see you," she said. "Just hold on there. I'm going to put you in. OK?"

"Oh yes, it's too OK!"

"You're a nice boy," she said as Modou moved up and down. "When you get to be a big boy, maybe two, three years, you can be my boyfriend."

"I will like that," said Modou. Then he spasmed with pleasure and collapsed with a sigh. "Oh Aja, you're too nice."

"Come now, Toofas," called Salif. "You finish, you move aside now."

Modou stood up and took his shorts and Umaru's in hand. "Ha! See this Umaru boy is too ready!"

Umaru lowered himself between the girl's legs and

finished in a minute. He stood up and began to dress. Modou held his own shorts in one hand. He lifted his t-shirt and said, "Look at this thing, Aja, he wants to play again. Just one more time, I beg."

Aja laughed and motioned with her hand. "Be fast now or Salif go charge you extra!"

Modou lowered himself down and bounced and wriggled until he convulsed again. Two other boys came up then and Modou rose and took his shorts from Umaru. They went and stood by the fire. Several more boys arrived, paid Salif and then stood waiting near Aja. Salif took Modou to one side and handed him a small backpack.

"Toofas, here my shoe doctor bag. I no go take it for village. You use it if you like, but keep it for me when I come back from village. OK?"

Modou took the pack. Inside were a few tins of shoe polish, a shoe brush, polishing rags, a large needle and strong thread, a bottle of shoe glue and some pieces of plastic and leather that could be used to repair shoes. He thanked Salif. He and Umaru called their thanks to Aja and departed.

"Umaru, sexing is too nice," said Modou as he and Umaru walked back down the beach.

"It's fine fine," agreed Umaru. "It's easy. Anyone can do it."

"When you're going in, oh, so soft, is nothing so fine," said Modou dreamily. "I want to be sexing all the time. Just sexing all day and all night, just stay right there."

"Mmm."

Modou grabbed Umaru's hand and held it to his crotch. "Feel this penis, he wants to be sexing again."

Umaru giggled and ran ahead, "Mine too!"

Modou caught him and they wrestled and grappled on the sand until they were tired.

They lay in silence then for a few minutes before they walked on down the beach

"Going to be a shoe doctor now," said Modou.

"It's good. You know how to be a shoe doctor?"

"No, but I'll find some boys to teach me."

Within a few days Modou was able to add shoe polishing and repairing as another source of income. But with ever more boys in the market every day it became increasingly difficult to earn enough to eat. Some days their best efforts won them only enough to buy a small loaf of bread, if that. Then they scrounged in the garbage for even small bits of food, moldy bread crusts and plate scrapings.

"Umaru," said Modou one night as they lay under their cloth beneath a fish market counter, "This life is difficult."

"Mmm."

"We got to be thinking how to better ourselves."

"Even one orange would make me better just now. My stomach is crying," groaned Umaru.

"Not just food. Got to be thinking about school, maybe. It's no good to just be market boys all the time."

"Who's going to pay school fees for us? Books? We don't even have money for food."

"We're not going to be staying like this always. We're going to be somebodies, Umaru," said Modou. "We're going to be somebodies one day."

A few days later their situation improved, because the police did another roundup of market boys. Modou and Umaru were just leaving the fish market after helping the fish vendors carry the morning catch when they heard shouting from further inside the market.

"It's a roundup," said Modou. He grabbed Umaru's arm. "Let's go."

They ran along an aisle leading to the main market road. Two policemen suddenly appeared at the end of the passage.

"You boys!" they shouted. "Stop!"

Modou glanced quickly around. The policemen were running toward them. He pulled Umaru into a stall and pointed to a back exit. "Go there and meet me later," he said. Then he jumped back out into the aisle, slid through the policemen's reaching arms and darted away in the opposite direction. Both policemen pursued him. He led them through the market until he was able to reach a main walkway.

Vendors laughed and shouted as he sped past. "Ho, Toofas!" they called and hooted at the police. He twisted around a couple of corners, darted into a narrow space between stalls and underneath counters in the next row to reach one of his private routes to escape from the market. The police rounded the corner after him and found that he had disappeared.

He located Umaru on the dunes above the beach and they crept through the long grass there and hid themselves in the swamp until late in the afternoon. The police were gone from the market and so were many of the boys they knew. But it was too late for them to earn any money to buy food that night so they went to their sleeping place hungry.

The next day they made enough money so that when they had eaten their fill they still had a few kuromas left over. Modou took one of the coins and put it in a zippered pocket on the side of the pack.

"This one is our bank," he said. "Every day we're

going to put small money there, for books, maybe even for school."

For a few days Modou was able to add to the bank every day but then they had several days when they had to use the money they had saved to buy food. This cycle repeated itself. The rainy season came and the bank remained empty for longer and longer periods of time. The boys were wet most of the time as well as hungry, but they survived.

The rains came less frequently and then stopped. With the advent of the dry season, boys started to come into the market from the countryside, since they were no longer needed on the farms. It became harder to earn or beg enough to live on and there was never any money in their bank.

Modou and Umaru sat side by side under a fish market counter in the darkness one night. They had not eaten since the previous day. Modou opened his shoe doctor pack. He took out the bottle of shoe glue and a plastic bag.

"That little Omar, today he showed me one thing to do when you are hungry," he said, mashing some of the shoe glue inside the plastic bag. He held the bag up to his face and puffed in and out a half dozen times, then coughed. "Oh!" He handed the bag to Umaru. "Do just like that," he giggled drunkenly. "You won't feel hungry any more."

"It's *genssing*," said Umaru. "I thought you said your *marabout* told you no *genssing*."

"Koran is saying no alcohol. *Genssing* is not alcohol so it's OK. Try it now."

Umaru took the bag and wrinkled his nose, "Is smelling bad."

"Just do like I say, you're going like it."

Umaru put the bag to his face and puffed in and out

several times and sneezed. Then he puffed several more times. "Oh!"

They fell against each other, laughing.

"This is very funny food," choked Modou as he lifted the bag to his face again and breathed the fumes. Then he allowed himself to slump backwards against the wall. He felt Umaru removing the bag from his hand and heard him puffing. They lost consciousness and drifted in and out of dreams. Whenever either awoke he reached for the bag and the welcome unconsciousness it provided.

"Toofas! Umaru! What you boys doing here?" said an angry voice.

Modou pulled himself out of a dream and groggily opened his eyes. One of the fish market ladies stood over him. He could not find any words to say.

"Ah!" she snorted in disgust. "You smelling glue! Stupid boys! Get out from here now!" She added emphasis to her words by kicking at the boys. They scrambled out from under the counter, stumbled toward the beach and collapsed against a log on the shore.

"Oh," moaned Umaru, "my head has a problem." He stared blearily out over the ocean.

"Head has a problem, stomach has a problem, nose has a problem, many, many problems," agreed Modou. Then he took a deep breath and coughed. He cleared his throat and inhaled deeply again. "*Genssing* is good, but we must have something to eat now now," he said decisively. He pulled himself to his feet, undressed and threw his clothes on the log. "Come, small boy, let's wash and then we'll go and find some food."

Umaru followed and when they were clean and dressed once again, they marched into the market, determined to find something to eat. Modou was called to deliver two messages almost immediately and earned enough to buy them a small loaf of the heavy local bread called *tapilapa*. They tore pieces off it and ate them while they continued to seek more work or food. By evening they had earned enough to share a plate of rice and fish before the market closed for the night.

They stopped sleeping in the fish market and sheltered from the wind behind their log on the beach. They used a piece of cardboard for a bed. Initially, they sniffed glue only at night, when driven to it by hunger. Then they began to sniff every night, whether they had eaten or not. They would inhale the vapors until they reached a dreamy state where everything was funny. They would roll around and play with each other and giggle. After inhaling a little more they would go inside to dreams of the past, where their mothers were smiling and their brothers and sisters were calling and laughing. A little more and unconsciousness would sweep over them in a wave.

They found that when the doors to the past were opened in dreams at night, they stayed open in the morning and they felt hopelessly sad and lonely when they awoke. They began to sniff in the morning then, to escape, and soon were seldom without bags of glue in their hands.

"This is not good," said Umaru one morning. "This is not good." Scabs from the solvent in the glue ringed his mouth.

"What you want, then?" muttered Modou.

"I don't know," said Umaru bleakly. "But this is not good."

"Why trouble me? If it's not good for you, it's your problem," snapped Modou. "Leave me be."

Modou applied the bag to his face and Umaru turned

away. Then he put his own bag to his face and inhaled deeply. Later they got up and staggered to the garbage dump at one edge of the market and scrounged and sifted for scraps of dirty food. They stopped speaking to one another except for grunts and were sprawled out unconscious on their piece of cardboard by mid-afternoon.

Modou heard rough voices through his stupor and cracked his eyes open. In the moonlight he could see figures moving around him. He attempted to raise himself but was too drunk to command his muscles.

"These boys *genssing* too much!" gloated a voice. "Let's see what they got."

Modou felt hands going through his pockets and tried to protest but found he could not speak, and when he thought, it did not seem to matter. As if through a fog he heard Umaru's voice protesting weakly.

"Look this pretty boy," said another voice that came from where Umaru lay. Modou tried to focus his eyes. He saw a big boy leaning over Umaru and pulling off his shorts. Umaru shouted and was answered by a couple of sharp slaps. Modou tried to lift himself up but was unable to do more than raise his arm feebly. The big boy flipped Umaru over onto his stomach and settled himself on top. Modou struggled to rise and stop Umaru's cries of pain but found he could not move or even speak. He closed his eyes and tried to blank out the sounds of Umaru being punched into submission. He felt his shoe doctor pack being pulled from under his head. When the voices went away, he managed to open his eyes. Umaru lay a few feet away, crying. Modou summoned a little strength to feel around for his glue bag. He found it and sniffed until Umaru's cries faded into the mist.

When Modou awoke he stared up into the gray morning sky and remembered what had happened the previous night. He felt nothing but an immense emptiness. Eventually his eyes sought the place where he had last seen Umaru. He sat up then and looked around. Umaru was sitting on his heels on the sand about ten meters away. He was hugging his knees, staring out at the ocean and rocking back and forth slowly.

Modou slumped down beside him.

"Oh Modou," said Umaru in a breaking voice, "I feel so bad."

Umaru suddenly seemed to Modou to be like a heavy weight pressing him down. Why should he feel bad because of Umaru?

"You're always complaining. It's not my problem," said Modou.

Umaru choked a sob and tears rolled down his cheeks.

"Be quiet now!" barked Modou. "You're always crying. You're stupid, stupid, stupid!"

Umaru's only answer was renewed crying.

Modou lunged at him and hit him across the face. "Cry for this then, you stupid! You just trouble me too much!"

Umaru scrabbled away wailing and crawled down the beach.

Modou ached with rage. The emptiness he had felt when he awoke had been replaced by cold anger and resentment and it was all Umaru's fault. He imagined the release of death. He stood up and walked down the beach away from Umaru, determined to find some way to kill himself. He was too tired to walk far and sat down on the sand. He fell on his side and stared at the grains of sand that were mixed with tiny pieces of shell, and felt utter loneliness and regret. He wished he could cry but he felt dead inside. The sun moved slowly across the sky and the silence was broken only by the desolate cries of gulls.

The crunch of sand underfoot told him of someone's approach. Modou felt a hand on his shoulder and looked up into Umaru's face.

"I'm sorry," said Umaru. "Modou, I'm sorry."

"Oh, Umaru," was all he could say.

Umaru stroked his head. "It's *genssing*. *Genssing* is very bad. Please say no more *genssing*."

Modou nodded. "No more *genssing*, never," he agreed. He pulled Umaru down so they lay with their heads on the sand. They looked into each other's eyes. "I'll never hit you again," Modou promised. "You OK?"

"OK now," answered Umaru. "Even if I die now, I'm OK."

"Maybe you like to hit me a little?" offered Modou.

"Maybe sometime," said Umaru. "Maybe put it in our bank for now."

"OK. Very good! I will make a deposit, one beating in the bank now, credit for Mr. Umaru. You can collect it any time. You hungry?"

"Two days now my stomach is on vacation."

"He's ready for work?"

"He's ready."

"You know, there's some baobab trees down inside the *bolong*. I am thinking the seeds are ready for picking. If we go pick some, maybe we can sell them to that woman who is making *booy*."

"Good idea."

They helped each other up then and brushed the sand off their clothes. Modou lay his arm across Umaru's shoulders. Umaru's arm wrapped around Modou's waist and they walked down the beach.

From: *The Masongala Daily Banner*

Street Boy Buildup?
By Jason Andrews

Masongala City Council officials are concerned at the increasing number of street boys in and around Manjako Market. "Our streets were clear of beggars for some time after the *talibés* were re-located but many of them have returned to the city as street boys now," said a MCC council member. "Some of them are working with stall holders in the market but many are just loitering, looking for a chance to steal something."

Another council member stated that many of these boys used rough language and were sniffing glue. This practice, known as "genssing," is reportedly widespread amongst the street boys. Sub-Inspector Ebu Ndiaye, Police Liaison Officer at the meeting, stated that the NPFD was concerned about the practice and was considering measures to limit the sale of the shoe glue, the substance most commonly abused. He also assured the MCC meeting that the NPFD planned to institute regular roundups of street boys in the near future. "This will discourage more boys from taking to the streets," he said.

Six

All was quiet in the early morning market except for the dusty scuffle of a pair of vultures fighting over some fish entrails. The blue-black sky was lightening on its eastern rim and soon the fishing canoes would be arriving on the beach with the night's catch. Underneath one of the cement counters in the fish market one of Modou's thin, brown arms snaked out of a tangle of rags and stretched up until it met the underside of the countertop. Then he sat up carefully so as not to hit his head and the coverings fell back to reveal Umaru, still curled up asleep. Modou leaned over and grabbed a feather caught in a crack of the cement. This he delicately passed over the the sleeping boy's nostrils. Umaru rubbed his nose. Then the feather dived into one ear and out again before the sleeper could brush it away.

"Modou! I'm sleeping."

"Come, small boy. The fishermen will be close to the beach now and we must hurry if we want to eat today."

"It's still night."

"No, it's day. Besides, I'm too hungry to sleep."

The boys padded through the empty market aisles until they reached the beach. Here the women who sold fish sat on the sand beside their empty plastic tubs, waiting for the fishermen in their great canoes. Modou and Umaru called greetings to the women and ran down to the shore to help beach the first canoe. The baskets of fish caught the dawn light and glistened rosy pink and silver. By the time the canoe was on the sand the women were at its side, exclaiming at the gleaming catch and bargaining with the fishermen. Another pirogue approached the shore and the boys walked into the water up to their hips to grasp its sides. They helped to pull it up until its bottom grated on the sand.

"Toofas!" called a woman as she filled her tub from the earliest canoe. "You will help me carry?"

"Today I go marry one beautiful girl," he cried. "How can I be carrying fish?"

All the women hooted.

"What woman so foolish go marry wicked boy like you?" called one.

"I am confuse!" shouted Modou. "Here on beach is too many beautiful young girls. I will to have to marry all!"

"Toofas, you should marry a donkey. Then this little Umaru would have at least one sensible parent."

"Is not my child. I found him in a tree and picked him like a coconut. How can a coconut have a donkey for a mother? You are very foolish girls. I no go marry any one of you today. Don't trouble me any longer."

"We are safe!" crowed one woman.

"Go cry in your house now," retorted Modou. "Maybe I will be feeling sorry for you tomorrow. You can come and rub my leg."

All the women hooted and laughed. Modou helped one woman lift her heavy tub and place it on her head then ran to another to help her sort her fish into two tubs. Umaru was already heading toward the market with a basin of fish balanced on a cloth pad on his head. Soon Modou, similarly burdened, followed him up into the fish market. The fishermen had thrown them a few fish for their help and the fish sellers gave them a few more. With these they trotted to the part of the market where the women who sold food were getting ready for the day. A woman who operated a small food shop eyed their fish disdainfully.

"You are having only *bonga*?" she said.

"Yes, Ma," said Modou, "but you know that *bonga* is the most tasty fish."

"But got one million bones," she said.

"Nice bones," insisted Modou. "Only small bones. Not going to cause problem. Peoples are enjoying, saying 'Only small bones here, is no problem.'"

The woman accepted their fish and said they could come back and have lunch later in the day.

"But oh Ma, we are so hungry now," begged Modou.

"Aieee. I have nothing now. But I saw bakery man go pass that way."

They ran and found the bread man and helped him to carry his long French loaves into the shops. He gave them one loaf of *tapilapa*, since it had fallen to the ground and was too dirty to sell. They ripped chunks from the loaf and chewed them while they walked down to the beach. There they dropped their tattered shorts and t-shirts on the sand and splashed and bathed in the cool water until their fingertips were ridged and wrinkled. Umaru sat down on a log to let the sun dry him while Modou danced calisthenics in front of him.

"I don't like clothes, you know. I think I am going to

be like a bush man," he said, bouncing up and down on his toes. He looked down past his belly and laughed, "You see, my penis is dancing!" He pulled on his shorts then turned and ran as fast as he could down the beach. Umaru watched him grow smaller and smaller and then larger and larger as he returned. He flopped down on the log beside Umaru, panting. "One day Umaru," he said, "I'm going to run like that and not stop, just run all the way to Europe or America. They will be seeing a big cloud of dust and saying 'What?'"

"And the police will have a big net for catching one half-naked African boy. They will say 'Ho, what kind of boy are you, running around like that? We'll take you to jail now for one long time.'"

"The *toubab* women will catch me first to enjoy me. Police are chasing me. Women are chasing me. I am letting the women catch me," said Modou. Then he stood up and said, "But now I am very hungry again. You know, stomach is not a good friend. You give him something and then he is just troubling you again soon soon. Let's go see what we can find in the market. You know, I think I am having an idea."

"Aieee! Trouble coming!"

"No, it's a nice idea. In this idea I am going to beat you seriously and you will be letting me, saying 'Oh Modou, now punch me a little here, and one more time here, please.'"

"It's a bad idea."

"No, it's sweet. You'll see."

Jason Andrews stepped out of a taxi in front of the market entrance, slung his backpack over his shoulder and looked up at the archway over the gate. The name was printed there in raised letters, along with the date when the market was built: Manjako Market - 1991. Traffic in front of this entrance was dense. White and green taxis crawled along accepting and disgorging passengers. Hawkers and shoppers eddied through the street and sidewalks in the morning sun between handcarts piled high with shoes and clothing and wheelbarrows full of oranges and mangoes.

Jason was not particularly tall though a little taller than most of the Africans around him. He was in his mid-twenties and had a vigorous growth of short blond hair above a square open face that still carried the curves of youth. He moved with the easy grace of an athlete. His loose cotton clothing was neat without being pretentiously so and the style suggested it was left over from years at university. He squinted up at the sky, wondering when he would lose the habit of checking the weather. In this part of Africa it was dry season now and, though he had been told there would be no clouds or rain for months, he still found himself looking up at the clear blue skies at least twice a day. Experienced expatriates had laughed at his interest in the weather when he had first arrived in Dazania. "Jason, there is no weather here," one had said. "They don't even have a weather report on the bloody TV. What are they going to say? 'Hot and sunny tomorrow. The three-day forecast? Hot and sunny. No rain expected for six months.'"

"Hot and sunny today," he said to himself with a smile of pleasure as a faint whiff of cooling breeze came through the market gates and riffled his loose cotton shirt. It carried the salt tang of the sea from the beach behind the market.

During the week he did most of his shopping at a Lebanese supermarket near his house in Casarica, the exclusive residential district where expatriates and rich Dazanians lived. On his small earnings as a freelance journalist he felt out of place in such a neighborhood, but the house and its staff of watchmen and a maid were less expensive than the bachelor apartment he had rented while he was a student in the USA. The payments he received for stories he wrote for a local newspaper did little more than meet his expenses but he was enjoying a sense of freedom and discovery. He had been in Dazania seven months now. He felt that he was beginning to understand national politics and had established good contacts that kept him briefed on the stories behind news.

He had formed the habit of spending Saturday mornings at Manjako Market because he never felt that he was truly in Africa so much as when he wandered through its crowded, busy aisles, with the smells of smoked fish and sawdust, the pyramids of mangoes, avocados and oranges and the good-natured cries of the salespeople. He liked Africa and because he had not expected to, this was a secret source of joy to him.

After loading his pack with purple onions, rice and a bundle of a spinach-like leaf, Jason left the main market road and passed into the shaded byways in search of a vendor selling shorts. Angry cries attracted his attention down a side aisle. In the shadows he could see two boys apparently engaged in a violent argument, with the smaller boy being brutally beaten. He strode quickly toward them and pulled the two apart. The larger boy lunged at the smaller, who sought shelter under Jason's arm. He fended off the larger boy.

"Here now!" he said as the bully struggled to get at his victim. "Stop it!" The small boy wrapped his arm around Jason's waist and peered out from under his arm. The bully circled toward his victim and they danced around in a circle, the small boy pulling and pushing Jason to keep him as a protective barrier, while the bigger boy jostled and grappled against him. Neither boy paid any more attention to him than if he were a part of the environment, a post or a pillar. He held the smaller boy under his arm and grabbed a handful of the other's t-shirt. They glared at each other.

"What's the problem here?" asked Jason.

"He go tief my money!" blurted the small boy resentfully. The bully looked away.

"Perhaps we should see if we can find a policeman to settle this..."

"Aieee," muttered the larger boy. Then he pointed his finger at the small boy, said something in the local language, twisted out of Jason's grasp and fled down the market aisle.

The thin shoulders beneath his arm moved and the hand unwrapped from his waist. "Thank you sir," said the boy. He still looked frightened.

"Are you OK?"

"Yes," said the boy slowly. "Thank you." Then he turned his big eyes toward Jason. "I go now." He took Jason's hand and shook it, then trotted away toward the center of the market, glancing fearfully backwards before disappearing into the mass of shoppers.

A little inflated with the sense of having prevented an injustice, Jason continued through the market until he had located the stalls where clothing was sold. When he had selected the pair of shorts he wanted and concluded the negotiations for price, he discovered that his wallet was missing from the back pocket of his trousers.

"Ah, you should not keep your money in your back pocket like that," said the man selling the shorts. "There are too many pickpockets here in the market. You should keep it in a front pocket and keep one hand in that pocket, like so," he demonstrated.

Jason nodded in chagrin and turned to leave. The shopkeeper insisted he take the shorts he had chosen. "You are living here—I see you every week. You can pay me for the shorts next time you come to the market. I trust you." This took some of the sting out of being conned by the two boys. As he walked toward the market exit though, he groaned inwardly at the thought of the problems he was going to have replacing his credit cards, driver's license and other documents. At least he had enough change in his pocket to pay the taxi fare back to his house.

He passed through the market gate and crossed the street, threading his way through the traffic to stand on the curb and flag a taxi going toward Casarica. Suddenly, above the din of taxi horns and hawkers' cries, he heard his name being called. He looked up to see a grinning boy perched on top of the market archway, that pickpocket boy, waving to him and dangling his skinny legs over 1991.

"Catch!" cried the boy and threw something toward him. It was his wallet, fastened shut with a thick elastic band. He opened it and found all his cards and most of his money. A piece of paper caught his eye and he unfolded it. It was a note, painstakingly printed in shaky primary school lettering.

> **Sir,**
> **I hop you ar wel. I am fin.**
> **You ar heving one stupid walit.**
> **It jus go jump into my han so.**
> **I punis him serusly.**
> **He beg plees tek 50 kuroma. He too hevi, no**

feel good.
I am kine boy. I am say yes ok but no mor
riding for bek poket. ok?
He say ok ok I go sit frant seat now.
The end.
MODOU

Jason looked up to the arch but the boy was gone.

"Dat one," said a nearby hawker, gesturing with his eyebrows toward the archway, "you no go catch 'im. He Toofas!"

"Too fast is he?" said Jason. "You know him?"

The hawker rearranged the socks displayed on his arm and smiled. "Ever'body know dat boy." He paused, glancing at the wallet. "He tief you?"

Jason looked up at the archway and smiled. "No," he said. "I just lost my wallet someplace. He returned it to me." He began to put the billfold where he habitually carried it, in his back pocket. Then he smiled to himself and said, "No, you go sit frant seat now," and put it into his front pocket.

In the evening, Modou and Umaru lay with their heads against a log on the beach behind the market. With his stomach full and the fifty kuroma bill from the *toubab* wallet crinkling in his pocket, Modou felt satisfied with the day, but Umaru was radiating an unusual tension. He sat up, hugged his knees and stared at his bare feet. Modou leaned sideways and nudged the boy with his shoulder.

"You angry?" asked Modou.

"No."

"OK. Sad?"

"Mmm."

"Tell me now."

"I don't like that, what we did today," said Umaru firmly.

"The *toubab*?"

"Mmm."

"It's just play, another kind of play."

"Not for him. We stole his money," said Umaru obstinately.

"These *toubabs* got too much money."

"I see his face now. I am feeling bad. He is having a good face. He was trying to help me and we took his money."

"OK. I gave his wallet back. You better now?"

"When we're working, when we're selling, when we're begging, I'm looking in the people's faces. It's OK. When we're playing like that, with that *toubab* today, it's not OK."

Modou sighed. "OK. I won't ask you to do that again. OK now?"

"Is you, is me, same thing," said Umaru sadly.

"Aieee! Little father, you are so difficult. OK. I promise. I won't do it. We won't do that any more. It's finished. OK now?"

"That fifty kuroma?" persisted Umaru.

Modou looked up to where the first stars were beginning to shine. "The peoples are saying, 'Oh that Umaru is a nice boy.' So ignorant they are. You are like a knife. OK, when we see that *toubab* again I'll give him back his money. OK now?"

"Mmm." They sat in silence for a minute.

"You angry?" asked Umaru.

"Small. You are talking true. When you say it I know it. But this life is hard. How're we going to better ourselves? We need money."

"Some people got no friend. That's hard."

"Some people got a friend and got money too."

"Now you're thinking, like a dog with a bone," said Umaru. "I am feeling easy now. My stomach is too happy. That woman cooks very good rice."

"Yes, full stomach is sweet. She is a good woman. But Umaru, that is a problem, too."

"Mmm," murmured Umaru.

"That is a good woman. When her business is not good and she has cooked rice left over, she feeds us well well. But when she has many customers she is saying, 'Sorry, boys.'"

"Well, then we are finding something else. We are eating nearly every day."

"It's not that, Umaru. It's that she is a good woman and we're happy if her business is bad. And we're hungry if her business is good. It's like we're on the wrong side of things."

"Mmm."

"You remember that big Demba?" asked Modou suddenly.

"You mean the one we knew here in the market?"

"Yes, with the crooked smile."

"Yes, he was nice," said Umaru. "Someone said he went out to the beach at Casarica. Long time past."

"I heard today he is gone to Europe, in a big plane."

"I'd like to fly in a plane like that. When you're in your seat one woman comes and gives you food and they show one video, and all the time you're flying, so high." Umaru laughed. "You remember that video we saw of people on plane and they were sexing in the small bathroom? These *toubabs* are very funny."

"And they have a lot of money," said Modou. "Demba met one *toubab* woman on the beach and she fell in love with him. Now she has carried him to Europe and he'll make big money there and come back here and drive around in a Mercedes-Benz."

"Maybe if he comes into the market he'll give us something nice. He'll say, 'Ah, Umaru and Toofas, my old friends, here, take this thousand kuromas and have a nice party.'"

"Yes, we'll still be here, hoping the good woman has a bad day," said Modou.

"Still thinking," said Umaru. He put his arm around Modou's shoulder and patted him. "This thinking trouble you have—maybe something is broke. Stomach is saying 'good' and head is saying, 'what?' Maybe your telephone is broke." Umaru tapped him on the side of the head and they tussled for a few minutes.

"And you know," said Modou, looking up at Umaru, who was seated on his belly, "Here in the market we're always looking, looking, looking—maybe policemen are coming for roundup again. It's not nice."

"What else are we going to do? We're only small boys."

"Maybe we should go out to Casarica, to that Makalo Beach with so many rich *toubab* tourists. Maybe I'll find one big yellow-hair *toubab* woman to love me. I will be pushing my nose on one nice white breast and sucking, mmm, and then poking my big thing…"

"And she is saying, 'Oh Modou, what is that little thing? I think one shrimp has fallen between your legs. Here, I go pick it for you.'"

"Don't worry. I am finding one small girl for you too, Umaru. She can play with your little worm until it gets big."

"But how're we going to eat? No fishermen at Casarica, no market."

"That's true, but money is there," said Modou with his hand on his chin, "I'm thinking."

"Let's go find our place to sleep. You can be thinking while we are walking. I want to sleep now."

One day Modou and Umaru were sitting on the beach picking over the remains of a smoked fish they had found. They had winkled out all the maggots and there were nice bits of good smoky-flavored flesh left amongst the bones.

"You know what's an orphan?" queried Umaru.

"Orphan is when you got no mother and father. We're orphans."

"I was hearing today about one nice place for orphans, called 'Sunnyvale Orphan Village.' Children there got a nice house, big compound, school, eating good food, nice uniform."

"Mmm," muttered Modou.

"I'd like to be having some shorts," said Umaru. His shorts had been stolen the previous day when he had taken them off to go swimming. He was wearing only an extra large t-shirt that hung down nearly to his knees.

"No-one is knowing you are naked," said Modou. "Nice big t-shirt. No problem."

"No problem for you. It's not your penis hanging in the wind."

"It's nice for penis. He wants to stand up? He is free, no shorts to cramp him up."

"Maybe they'll give me some shorts if we go to that place."

"That was good fish," said Modou, licking his fingers.

"I'd like to have two more fish like that," said Umaru. "You like to go see that orphan place?"

"I think I am having one free afternoon," said Modou. "You know where it is?"

"They are saying it's in Kokonka. A little bit far."

It took them three hours to walk to Kokonka. People along the way pointed them toward their destination.

"They got one high wall here," said Modou as they followed it along the road, "like prison." The wall was twelve feet high with broken glass and curls of barbed wire along the top. "Must be many people trying to get out."

"Maybe it's people trying to get in," said Umaru. "Gate is up ahead there."

"Sunnyvale Orphan Village, orphans is coming!" cried Modou.

There was an unfriendly looking gatekeeper guarding the tall, iron gate. Through its bars they could see children walking around and playing and many well kept buildings. The gatekeeper looked at them suspiciously.

"We're orphans," said Modou.

"Me too," said the gatekeeper.

"You're a big orphan. We're small orphans. Like to go inside and talk to the peoples."

"Got paper?"

"What paper?"

"No paper, no go inside."

"What paper? We're orphans. Orphans got no paper. Look you this boy," said Modou pointing to Umaru. "He got no pants, how he go have paper?"

"You must have paper for prove you orphans. Maybe your parents just tired of dirty boys like you, send you here to get education. Here is only for cer-ti-fied orphans."

"Let us in for talk with the peoples," said Modou.

"No paper, no go inside. Europeans are having this place. Tell me 'Gatekeeper, someone is coming with government car, bringing children with paper, you go let them in. Anybody else is stay outside.'"

"Where we go get paper?"

"Government."

"Where is government?"

"Masongala." The gatekeeper gestured with his chin.

"I was wrong," said Modou as they loitered their way back toward Masongala. "We're not orphans."

"What are we then?"

"We're just nobodies. We're nothing."

On the way back to the market they found on the dusty roadside a pair of underpants with only one big hole in the back. In the market Umaru washed them under a standpipe and put them on.

"Looking good!" said Modou. "You got a backlight there but front is like new. Going to have the women chasing you now."

On the opposite side of Masongala from the market was a building with a sign that read, "Street Children Rehabilitation Center." Early one day they met a man in the market who said they should go there. It was only an hour's walk so they decided to take a look at it later in the day.

When they arrived at the building they spoke to the doorkeeper. "What's that, 'Re-hab-il-it-ation?'" asked Modou.

"Is where they fix you up, make you like new, like a laundry—now you all wrinkled up and dirty. Rehabilitation go make you nice and clean, iron go get out all wrinkles," said the gatekeeper. He smiled, "It's good for boys like you, go inside and talk to the woman."

"Maybe we don't need to be 'cer-ti-fied' for street children," whispered Umaru hopefully as they entered the compound. Inside, a few boys were kicking a football back and forth and another boy was washing his clothes in a basin by a standpipe. The gatekeeper pointed towards a small house just inside the entrance to the right and said, "Office is there."

A young African woman sitting behind a desk gave them a nice smile when they stood before her. There was another desk and several tables in the room. One of the tables had a partially completed jig-saw puzzle of kittens playing with a ball of wool. A bookcase filled with tattered books and magazines stood against one wall. Down a hall-way were two doors labeled Examinations and Dispensary. Modou said someone told them to come there, that there was something for street boys.

"You are welcome," said the young woman. Then she told them all about the program, how they would sleep in dormitory housing and eat every day and be trained in a trade so they could become useful members of society.

"Sounds good," said Modou. "We are coming in."

The lady seemed happy but said she had to warn them that the program was very demanding and many children and youths were not ready.

"We ready for lunch and after be learning trade. Is good," said Modou.

"Yes, well, children and youths who want to join the program must be prepared to make a commitment."

"No problem if I am knowing what is commitment."

"We have to have rules, you know, like no drugs."

"We are not eating drugs."

"Well, you all say that, but we're not fools here. Living in the street, we know you're probably doing drugs and before you can be a part of this program, you have to face that fact. You have to face up to the fact that you are addicted. Until you face that fact, until you freely admit it, we can't begin to help you."

"OK," said Modou. "We doing *genssing*, before before. But not now. OK?"

The woman smiled. "I suppose it's possible," she said.

Modou turned his eyes down and bowed his head, "You too much smart," he said meekly. "We must have help for stop smelling drugs."

"You do understand," said the woman triumphantly. "That's the first step in the right direction."

"Not just me, Umaru too. Look him. His head full up with glue." Umaru's wide-eyed and startled expression seemed to fit Modou's description and the woman assured them that they would soon be getting help. Then she read them a long list of things they must do and things they must not do to be part of the program.

"No problem," said Modou.

Then she asked them a lot of questions: their names, how old they were, where they were from, how long they had lived in the streets and many other questions. She noted all their answers carefully on paper forms.

Finally she looked up and said, "Well, that's about it, then. Of course you'll have to see one of our workers for interviews but I think we may be able to find spaces for you both."

Modou and Umaru exchanged grins.

"Unfortunately," continued the young woman, "our programs are funded by overseas sponsors. That means we have to find someone who is willing to pay for your participation in the program. Right now we have a bit of a waiting list so you cannot come into the program immediately. What you will have to do is to check in here every day or so to see if we have found sponsors for you. When we get sponsors then you can move out to the farms and start your training."

"How long 'til we go begin?" asked Modou.

"Probably within a month or two at most. Modou, you qualify to be in our Youth Trainee Program. You would be living in the YTP dormitory near Kalata. It's a very nice big farm with a well-equipped workshop. And Umaru, I think we can find a place for you in our children's program at Talangi. It's very nice there. It has a farm also and there are many other young children for you to play with. Now…"

"We no go stay for same place?" asked Umaru.

"Oh no, we always keep the big boys separate from the smaller children to prevent abuse. It's necessary, I'm afraid. But several times each year we have joint program activities and you might get to see each other then, in a controlled environment."

"We staying together all the time," said Modou.

"But you see, at your age we classify you as a youth. And this little fellow here, though he's only a few years younger than you, he falls into the child category."

"Maybe he older," said Modou. "You know we are not knowing age correctly."

"No, I'm sorry. I think you gave me the correct information. You will have to go into separate programs. But you're not even related; what difference does it make? In a few months you will have lots of new friends and we have excellent professional counselors to help you get over any emotional problems or traumas you may have."

"We have to stay for different places?" asked Modou slowly.

"Yes, I'm afraid so," said the woman. The boys exchanged a glance.

"We always go stay together for one place," said Modou. Umaru nodded.

"I'm afraid it's not possible," said the woman.

"Too bad," said Modou and gazed around the room. "Is any food here?"

"No, I'm afraid we don't have any feeding program here," she said apologetically.

Modou and Umaru turned and walked towards the door.

"I'll save your forms," called the woman. "When you're prepared to make a commitment, come back and see us. You're always welcome."

"Not even lunch!" said Modou once they were outside. "No breakfast and long walk here and now long walk back." He groaned, "Stomach program is needing re-hab-il-it-ation. Aieee. I am falling into dead body category."

Umaru said, "You just sit down here, Modou. I am coming." Then he kicked his bare foot hard against the wall of the Street Children Rehabilitation Center and began to cry and limp down the street. He came to a small store and the woman there came out and dried his tears and quieted his sobbing. Five minutes later he hobbled back with a loaf of *tapilapa* bread. They sat on the edge of the road and ate it.

"You're a very foolish boy," sighed Modou with satisfaction. He patted his belly and wrapped his arm around Umaru's shoulder.

"Mmm. I should be smashing my hand. To be smashing my foot when there is a long walk is not smart. You should be telling me these things."

"You are not walking well?" asked Modou.

Umaru sniffed and surveyed his cut and swollen foot. "I think it's broke."

"I am having a 'carrying children on back' program. You like to join that program?"

Umaru laughed, "I think I am having a 'riding on back' program. You like to join that program?"

"I'll join your program if you join mine."

After Modou carried Umaru piggyback down the street for a few minutes he said, "I think this is what that lady is calling 'joint program activities.'"

"It's OK, but I like to be a little closer to you. It's not a separate program," said Umaru, lacing his arms around Modou's neck and hugging him tightly.

"You making a commitment?" laughed Modou.

"What is that? Commitment?"

"Something you make, maybe like chair or table. Carpenter is making chair. Youth Trainee is making commitment. You need one commitment? Bring hammer. Bring nail. I go make one nice commitment for you now now."

"I like that," said Umaru dreamily, his chin resting on Modou's shoulder. "You go make one for me."

"OK. But not today. Maybe tomorrow. Today I am busy with 'joint program activities.'"

From: *The Masongala Daily Banner*

MCC to Fine Donors
By Jason Andrews

Masongala City Council today passed a bylaw making it illegal for people to give money or food to street children.

Mayor of Masongala, Ousman Ceesay, said "People are kind-hearted but don't realize that giving money or food to beggars just encourages them. After a while street children realize that they can live well on the street and they become reluctant to go back to their homes."

In a prepared statement, City Council stated that the steady increase in the number of street children is a direct result of people failing to recognize the harm that misplaced generosity does. Charitably minded people are invited to donate to the MCC Indigent Center, the officially sanctioned agency for support of the genuinely homeless of Masongala. The center currently has the capacity to house and feed twenty needy persons.

Mayor Ceesay said that both the Dazanian National Army and the NPFD have been requested to help to ensure this bylaw is respected. Organizations and businesses that persist in giving handouts will face legal action or closure.

From: *The Masongala Daily Banner*

NPFD to Clean Up Street Boy Problem
By Jason Andrews

Inspector-General of the NPFD today warned street boys to stay off the streets and out of the markets from now on or risk being relocated back to their villages. He stated that the NPFD was not going to sit by idly while the number of street boys increases. "We must stamp this problem out before it becomes serious," he said.

A senior police official said that the new relocation program was being sponsored by the Rights for Kids Coalition and that street boys would be relocated to their home areas and re-united with their families in accordance with guidelines laid down during the Darra Children's Relocation Program.

RKC Country Program Director, Reba Brecken, speaking in support of the program also expressed concerns about increasing drug use amongst street children. "Until we have legislation to control these substances," she said, "the most effective way to curb drug use is to remove the children from the environment where they are likely to be tempted."

The Ministry of Health and Social Welfare is said to be preparing a bill that will severely limit the sale of shoe glue, the substance most widely abused by street boys.

Seven

The hum of the air conditioner muted the incessant honking and shouting in the streets below Reba's office and gave her a sense of efficiency and control over her environment. Inside, the décor was subdued; just one calm art deco print of a single lily adorned the cool blue walls. The Danish Modern office furniture she had chosen, while it was comfortable, was similarly simple and clean-lined. She felt it was quite Spartan. Reba sat at her desk and flicked through the pages of the project proposal while she listened to the young man explain his plans.

"Some of their worst problems are because their diet is bad," said Mr. Cham. "Often even when they are given food in the streets, it is not good food, not anything like a balanced diet—and most suffer from some kind of skin infection because they have no way to keep themselves clean."

Mr. Cham had come to the RKC offices hoping to raise some money for the project he was managing, a modest drop-in center for street children. Currently he was able to offer a small number of street children one meal several times per week. He wanted to expand his feeding program to at least one meal per day and wished to install showers behind the old two room building he was renting, so the street children could bathe.

"You know, Mr. Cham, this is wonderful work you are doing. Street children need so much. But I don't see any counseling component in this proposal. We believe that one of the greatest needs of children in difficult circumstances is counseling. We are hearing reports lately of increased drug use among street children. I should think substance abuse counseling should be a high priority in those circumstances. And, of course, they must have help to deal with the traumas of being abused, of being alone and unwanted, of having to beg for their most basic needs. Soap and water is fine, but the psychological damage they have suffered is much harder to heal."

Mr. Cham's was not the first such proposal that had passed across her desk. People just did not understand that there was no point in simply providing material supports unless they were part of a larger program of raising community awareness, counseling, family re-integration, government lobbying and a planning framework that would integrate all these activities within the larger context of children's rights.

"Oh, these children are not much troubled by psychological problems," said Mr. Cham. "Mostly what they need is food and a place where they can get cleaned up and have their little medical problems treated. Many of them right now are suffering from scabies and ringworm."

Really, thought Reba, here was the perfect example of a good-hearted person just not aware of the deeper aspects of the problem he was so lamely trying to solve. "Surely the demeaning experience of having to beg for the barest necessities must cause psychological damage to any child," she said, peering at him over the tops of her reading glasses.

"You must be filled with pride to be demeaned by asking for help," said Mr. Cham. "Our children are very humble. It doesn't disturb them to ask adults for assistance. That is part of their role as children. As adults, our role is to help them however we can. And that is why I have come to you."

"Hmm," murmured Reba as she flipped past a few more pages of his proposal. "Ah, I don't see any statistics here in your proposal. It is usual to have a clearly defined target population. I mean, if you don't know how many children you are dealing with, how can you possibly plan ahead to ensure that you have sufficient resources?"

"There are too many. Everything we can provide is thankfully received. But there are so many we are not able to help. We are feeding about fifty children now but there are hundreds more who would come if we had more food to give them."

"It's not within RKC policies to provide food or other material supports under normal circumstances. We believe that long-term solutions can only come from the community and that to intervene with material supports simply leads to a prolongation of the process." Mr. Cham's shoulders sagged and he sank a little lower in his chair. "But there are other agencies that may help you," she said, trying to be helpful. "Have you talked to the people at the World Food Program?"

"Oh yes," said Mr. Cham. "They were very sympathetic. But all their resources have already been allocated to the government's feeding program in the primary schools. They said they would consider our application in their next five-year plan. But they're only in the second year of the current five-year plan." Mr. Cham decided there would be no point in mentioning that much of the WFP rice and oil supplies were for sale in the markets and that many school principals privately viewed the program as a valuable means of supplementing their meager salaries.

"What about your own Ministry of Health and Social Welfare—surely this is the kind of project they might be interested in supporting?"

"I went there first. And they were very understanding and agreeable. But you know, in our government's desire to qualify for international loans, those IMF/World Bank loans, funding for social welfare programs was severely cut back. They asked me if we would not consider changing our project to a crèche for abandoned infants. They feel that street children at least have some ability to take care of themselves but their department has no facilities to care for unwanted babies. Indeed the social welfare officer I spoke to was quite harassed with all the babies she was receiving. You know, baby-dumping is becoming a serious problem."

"Mr. Cham, I think what you are trying to do is very worthy and I will pass along your proposal to our head office. But to be honest with you, I can't offer much hope. International agencies such as RKC have to keep a global perspective and have to explore long-term solutions and means of effecting change. They are not generally willing to support projects such as this. We promote children's rights because we believe genuine solutions can only be found within that framework. This doesn't seem to be a high priority with your project. And that's fine for you, I understand what you are trying to do, but there's no promotion of children's rights, no advocacy, no awareness raising, no WID or environmental components…"

Mr. Cham looked around the room as if help might be found on the walls. "WID?" he said doubtfully.

"That's Women In Development," said Reba. "And how about community participation? What is the community doing to support your project?"

"We do have one bakery man who gives us bread sometimes and there's one Lebanese merchant who regularly gives us a bag of rice." Mr. Cham was grasping at straws. "And a merchant gave me some flip-flops only this morning."

"That's good," said Reba without much conviction, while making a few notes in the margin of Mr. Cham's proposal.

"Ms. Brecken," said Mr. Cham as he sat up and leaned forward, "I can also appreciate your point of view. But for me it's simple. What good is it to have these children's rights to food established, if we cannot provide food for them to eat? They can't eat rights. They must have food."

"Ah, but you see, Mr. Cham, that's just where you're going wrong. All we can do as agents of change is to help governments to implement and enforce policies. The responsibility of fulfillment, of providing material supports, that's not our responsibility. And if we are ever to effect meaningful change, we cannot accept it as our responsibility. It's the community's responsibility. As long as we keep on pumping in our resources, we are just encouraging them to continue to evade their responsibilities."

Mr. Cham looked down. He flicked with his fingernail at a bit of lint on his trousers. When he looked up he seemed somehow older. It made Reba feel quite generous. She reminded herself that here was a man who at least was in touch with the problem, even if his misguided enthusiasm could have little effect. "You know," she said, "I think you have some good ideas here but they need to be fleshed out a little. Why don't you leave this proposal with me until

I have a chance to make some notes on it? Come in next week, if you can, and then maybe we can re-write some parts of it together. Sometimes we can allocate funds for basic needs, as long as this support is in the proper context. And sometimes some of the embassies have funds available for charitable projects like this. I'll ask around and see what I can find."

"That's very kind of you. Thank you."

"You know, there's one other question I have to ask you."

"Yes?"

"Your name, 'All God's Children,' implies some religious affiliation to your organization."

"We wanted to make the point that these street children are God's children, that they deserve what every child deserves…"

"You might want to consider changing the name—you know RKC and many other modern agencies don't really approve of religious proselytizing of any kind—we believe that children should be free to choose their beliefs without being seduced by material offerings."

"Oh, no. There is nothing like that – we don't talk to the children about any religion. There is no hidden religious agenda. We just wanted our name to say to people that these children deserve to be well treated."

"I'm glad to hear that, but you might think about changing the name – it does suggest a religious affiliation."

"Thank you, Ms. Brecken. I'll tell our board of directors what you have said. I don't think any of us thought that our name would have any negative meanings."

"Come and see me next week." She consulted her diary. "Say on Tuesday afternoon, at two o'clock, and we'll see if we can find some way to work together."

When Mr.Cham arrived at the All God's Children drop-in center he found two boys waiting for him.

"Aha! Toofas and Umaru. Salaam Alaikum!

The boys returned his greeting, "Alaikum as-Salaam!"

"You know I am always happy to see you, but today I'm sorry there is no food here."

"It's not food, sir," said Modou. "It's Umaru's foot. It has some problem."

"Oh yes, I see." Umaru's right big toe was deeply cut and infected. "It's very badly swollen. It must be painful."

He opened the gate to the compound and invited them inside. A few minutes later the toe had been liberally doused with hydrogen peroxide, cleaned and bandaged. So many of the street children suffered from wounds that were neglected that when he bandaged them, Mr. Cham always took the opportunity to teach them a little. "When you have some wound like this you must clean it up immediately, you know. And then wrap it up in a piece of clean cloth so it stays clean. Then it won't get infected and all swollen up like this. If it is clean it will heal quickly. You understand?"

The boys nodded. "Thank you sir."

"And, going around the streets with no shoes is bad for your feet. There are pieces of glass all over the place and you will always be cutting your feet. Look, I have something for you. One kind man today brought me some plastic slippers to give to you children. Here is a pair for each of you."

The boys slipped the flip-flops on and were thanking him again when there was a loud banging on the compound gate. Mr. Cham peered through the window, then pushed the boys out the rear door of the house and pointed to the back wall of the compound.

"Run and jump over the wall quickly," he whispered. "There are many soldiers outside."

They were over the wall in a few seconds. Then they crouched to peer through a crack. Mr. Cham opened the compound gate and several soldiers burst in pushing him backwards and shouting at him. Another soldier entered with the All God's Children sign in his hands.

"Aieee!" whispered Modou. "That's Major Esse! I've seen his picture in the newspaper."

Major Esse pointed at the small outside kitchen shed where food was prepared for the street children. Two soldiers began smashing down the walls and throwing all the plastic plates and dishes and aluminum pots into a pile in the center of the compound. Two other soldiers went into the house where Mr. Cham had his first aid and other supplies. They carried out the few pieces of furniture and the first aid kit and piled them with the cooking equipment.

Major Esse was talking and shouting at Mr. Cham while his soldiers were smashing everything. The boys could only hear the shouts, "Stupid Man! You're only making the problem worse!" The Major threw the sign on top of the pile and a soldier set it on fire. Another of the soldiers began to circle inside the compound wall, looking for other things to destroy. The boys ran away for fear they would be discovered.

The next day, Modou sensed danger when he spied two police officers strolling down the main market road. Something about the way they were walking and eyeing everyone sharpened his perceptions. He glanced around and saw two more uniforms sauntering down the aisle where he and Umaru walked. The police quickened their pace when they saw the boys. Modou pulled Umaru into a stall.

"It's a roundup!" he said. "Go through the back of this stall here and follow along our special path, you know, the one that goes over the food sellers and behind the fish market. I'll meet you at the edge of the *bolong* as soon as I have a little race with these policemen."

Umaru nodded and ducked out the back of the stall. Modou had rehearsed this escape with him so many times that he knew exactly where to go. Modou drifted idly out the front of the stall. The policemen were about thirty feet distant.

"You boy!" one called. "Stop now."

"No thank you," cried Modou and sped down the aisle with the shouting policemen in pursuit. Two more policemen blocked the end of that route. He swerved into a market stall, jumped through a window at the back and raced along a lane that joined the main market road. He leaned into the turn to enter the wider passage, and two more police leaped into pursuit. They yelled, "Toofas!"

The market vendors picked up the cry and began to shout, "Toofas! Toofas!" Many bystanders jeered his pursuers. As he careened down the main market artery, shoppers and sellers moved to the sides and began to cheer, "Toofas! Toofas!" People in the crowded aisles ahead picked up the cheer and vendors began to beat the rhythm on the sides of their stalls. "Toofas! Toofas! Toofas! Toofas!"

Several more police officers pushed their way through the crowd and stepped into sight blocking his route barely fifty feet away. Modou was trapped, six behind him and others up ahead. He jumped onto a market stall counter and hoisted himself up onto the rusty iron sheets that sheltered large parts of the market from the sun and rain. He felt a policeman's hand grasp his heel but he twisted free and raced clattering across the patchwork of roofs, leaping over gaps above the aisles. Sometimes he and Umaru had played tag on these roofs, raising the anger of the shop-keepers below as dust rained down on their wares. But now those same shopkeepers shouted his name with glee when they glimpsed him bounding from roof to roof. "Toofas! Toofas! Toofas! Toofas!" shouted the crowd joyfully and the market rang with his name as he sailed across the sheets of tin and plywood. Modou spread his arms like wings as he swooped towards two vultures perched in his way and laughed as they scrabbled to one side.

He sprang the gaps and sped toward the fish market that backed onto the beach. But when he reached the last alley, he stopped. It seemed too wide to jump. A dozen policemen charged into the passage below, preventing him from dropping down from the roof. He measured the distance with his eye. The crowd fell silent. He ran back, turned, then raced to the edge and soared over the heads of the policemen. They flailed their sticks and shouted in rage. The crowd burst into a cheer as he landed on the fish market roof. The market women ululated, danced and clapped and the male vendors chanted, "Toofas! Toofas! Toofas! Toofas!" and drummed on their countertops.

He jumped down to the ground on the beach behind the fish market. Policemen poured out of the market onto the sand. Modou grinned. Now they could not trap him. Now it was only a matter of running.

Umaru was hidden in the mangroves at the edge of the *bolong*, the mangrove swamp that lay along the coast for twenty-five kilometers between the city and the tour-ist beaches. The mangrove trees here were little more than bushes, generally less than two or three meters high. They squatted above the mud on many visible roots like spiders' legs. The roots, which were underwater at high tide, came together where they rose above the tidewater to form a short trunk that divided almost immediately into many small branches. This dense low growth, shallow salty water and mud were the *bolong's* main characteristics but numerous shifting tidal watercourses wound their way through the swamps and the edges of these were sometimes dry and sandy. Except in these sandy areas, walking was difficult and the *bolong* was a favored refuge of criminals. The police were reluctant to enter there and even if they did mount a search in the *bolong*, it was easy to evade them.

Behind the cover of some clumps of mangrove Umaru watched the beach for Modou and when he saw him he laughed. Ten policemen ran barely fifty meters behind him. Umaru knew Modou was just playing with them, running much more slowly than he could, just to tease them into chasing him.

As soon as Modou saw the *bolong* he accelerated and the policemen were left far behind. Once when watching a television in a shop window, he and Umaru had seen the winner of a big race raising his hands and making Vs with his fingers as he crossed the finish line. Modou lifted his arms and made the same sign just before he vaulted across the tidal stream that marked the edge of the swamp. He plunged into the undergrowth and Umaru struggled through the mangroves to join him. They pushed their way further into the bush but stopped to peer through the tangle of leaves and branches as the policemen came panting up to the edge of the swamp.

The police stood with their hands on their hips and stared into the dense brush. One of them cupped his hands over his mouth and yelled, "Toofas! I know you. Next time we go beat you seriously."

"You no go catch me never!" shouted Modou. "You too fat! You too much fat for run." Umaru pulled on his sleeve to make him quiet.

"You go die, Toofas," roared the enraged policeman. He leaned sideways trying to spy the boy. "I'm warning you!"

"You go die first! You old man!" came Modou's voice from the bolong. "Go home now. Go to bed. Take some rest. When you dead I go sex your wife!"

Umaru dragged Modou away and they fled further into the maze of mangrove and mud, giggling and stumbling as they ran. The police turned their backs and walked stiffly toward the market, hoisting their belts and fanning themselves with their visored hats.

The boys came to a low dune where tidal waters created a long gently flowing pool. "Let's swim," said Modou and dropped his clothes on the sand. They washed the mud off their legs and lolled in the warm shallow water.

"That policeman was very angry," laughed Modou. "Tonight I think he'll beat his wife."

"It's very nice to be insulting policemen, but it's not a small thing," said Umaru. "When we go back to the market they'll be watching, watching, watching for us. They won't wait for roundup again. They see you, they're going chase you. Every time."

"We're not going back to the market, Umaru. Market is finish. Now we're going to Kadanka Bay and that Makalo Beach. Going to be rich! Find us some nice *toubab* women with big breasts."

"This *bolong* is very big. Where is that beach?"

"It's no problem. I am knowing one man. He was

telling me about the *bolongs*. You see the way this water is moving?

"Mmm."

"The tide is going out now so this water is moving toward the ocean. We just walk along the sand now and follow the water. Soon we'll see the ocean. Then we just follow this bad beach until we come to the tourist beach. It's simple."

"It's a little bit far I think."

"You want to stay here? Come, let's go now. If we are walking seriously we will be there tonight."

Police Quell Market Riot
By Jason Andrews

Police put down what they referred to as a 'civil disturbance' yesterday in Manjako Market. Only a few casualties were reported and no arrests were made.

The riot is said to have arisen during one of the regular police collections of street children for relocation to the provinces. Apparently there is one street child living in the market who always succeeds in evading capture during these activities. His escape yesterday was more memorable than usual.

Eyewitnesses claim that the boy, called "Toofas," teased, outwitted and outran police from one end of the market to the other, then made his final escape by flying across the roofs of the market like a bird. His present whereabouts are unknown but the popular sentiment is that he will never be captured.

The NPFD spokesman described such reports as nonsense. He said that vendors caused the disturbance when they were scolded for harboring street children in their shops and that order was speedily restored through disciplined action by the NPFD.

Eight

The first day that Modou and Umaru spent on Makalo Beach the tourist police chased them. After they had escaped they met another boy in the bush where they were hiding.

"You can't just come to this beach like ragged beggars," said the boy. "The tourist police will run after you every time and if they catch you…" he wagged his hand, "…aieee, you will suffer. Come with me. I'll take you to one woman who will help you."

They became sellers of water. Every morning they went to the woman's house. She had a refrigerator and a freezer. There they would load up a Styrofoam cooler with plastic bags of frozen water for Africans and some tap water in mineral water bottles for Europeans. The box kept the ice from melting too fast and the ice kept the water cold. The woman loaned them clean shorts and t-shirts to wear so the police would not harass them.

When they had lived in the market, Modou had observed the sellers' methods, the friendly cajolery, and the patience and persistence. When Modou combined these tactics with his own brand of wit and the merry light in his eyes, his water sold like it was in short supply. There was seldom anything left in their box when they returned to the woman's house in the evening. Modou and Umaru made friends with the tourist police and gave them a little money and free water from time to time. Soon the boys had made enough to outfit themselves in new clothes and were eating well every day.

"Modou," said the woman one day. "You selling more water than other boys. How you sell so much water? You bought some kind of charm from *marabout*?"

"No Ma, you know the secret? Is not me, is our team— Umaru and me. I am talking. The *toubabs* are laughing— they are on vacation, they want to have a good time. They want to play a little, to be joking, but they are a little bit afraid. Maybe Africans is going to bite them or some bad thing. Then they are looking at Umaru and they are not afraid any more. He so small and funny looking, not going to bite anyone. And bad thing? His face say he don't even know how to think bad thing. They are thinking there is nothing for fear, so they are buying."

"Is true. I see it."

"We are working so hard for you. Every day we bring you so much money and then you just give we small small."

"Be quiet. Is very cost to do business like this. Look you my fridge. Very cost. And the electricity it eats, you have no idea. If it breaks I must pay mechanic to repair. There is no end of trouble. You are very lucky I give you so much. Some times even I am losing money when I am giving to you."

"Yes, Ma." said Modou.

While examining a hotel rubbish pile one day the boys found a large cardboard box from a new refrigerator. They carried it to the bush behind the hotels where they usually slept and it became their "house." They lay there one night under the piece of cloth they used for a blanket.

"This beach is very good," said Umaru.

"Yes, we are eating and we have our house so we are keeping a little bit clean now, but…"

Umaru laughed, "You're thinking. When you talk so I know you're thinking."

"I can't help it—it's like my brain is itching and when I scratch it, ideas keep falling out. You see, I'm happy with this beach too. Here we're on the right side of things, not like at the market. But you know it's still just same same. How much money you got?"

Umaru fingered the change in his pocket. "Maybe one kuroma."

"Give me."

"No!" giggled Umaru.

They wrestled lazily for a few minutes. Modou put Umaru's coins together with his own. "You see, we have only three kuromas. Tomorrow we buy some small bread for breakfast and we have nothing. Every day same same. Start with nothing. End with nothing. We make enough to buy food but no more."

Umaru leaned over and scratched Modou's head.

"What?"

"Itching brain." He burrowed into Modou's shoulder and sniffed. "Aieee, you are smelling."

"You are not a nice boy. I am lying here trying to think but everywhere is Umaru smelling. I am not saying anything. No. I am a nice boy, but you, you are a very rude boy to say I am smelling when your bad smell is like to kill my nose."

Umaru giggled sleepily.

"Tomorrow we must find small soap and go down the beach far far so we can wash our clothes."

"Mmm."

"But Umaru, I'm thinking, you know sometimes we are selling, selling, selling, and the people are enjoying, they are laughing, but they don't want any water. Europeans don't want that bag water and they are worrying that the bottle water is from tap. I'm thinking maybe we can be having something else for the people to buy, so every time I'm talking, you know, I'm selling something. If they are not wanting water, then I am having something else for them. I'm tired of selling, selling, selling, and then just giving all the money to that woman." He thought for a minute. "You know that store where we buy our bread in the morning? The one owned by the Mauritanian?"

There was no answer. He listened to Umaru's deep regular breathing then snuggled down beside him. "Well, sleepy boy, tomorrow I'm going to talk to that store man. You know he just comes down from Mauritania to do business. Businessman! Is business now!"

In the morning Modou woke with the clear sweet whistle of the Barbary Shrike in his ear. He listened until the little bird's mate answered and the echo died away in the trees. It had a sound like gold and he knew he was going to be lucky that day.

When Modou made his proposition, the Mauritanian storekeeper grunted and called for his father. A few minutes later the old man came out. He stared at Modou while his son explained what Modou wanted. He asked his son a few questions in their own language and then he nodded.

"OK," said the son, "We go give you six today."

"Cold ones!" said Modou.

"OK. Cold ones, what kind?"

"Three Fanta, three Coca Cola."

"You bring back bottles and pay nice nice, we go give you more tomorrow."

They tucked the soft drinks among the bags of ice and plastic bottles of water. Umaru helped Modou balance the Styrofoam box on his head and they strode toward the beach.

"This is foolish. You said we're going to pay full price to the store man. How're we going to make any money?" asked Umaru.

"Think like a businessman, Umaru. Five kuromas is full price for the Mauritanian. On the beach, I think full price is ten kuromas."

"Who will pay ten kuromas when everyone knows the fix price is five kuromas?"

"*Toubabs! Toubab* tourists don't know if one Coca Cola is three kuromas or five kuromas or ten kuromas or twenty kuromas. No fix price on the beach. If we say price is ten kuromas, price is ten kuromas."

Business was good. They sold all their stock on the first day and carried more on following days. Each morning after visiting the water lady and collecting their box and bags of ice, they went to the store and filled all the available space with bottles of soft drinks. They did not sell so much water but their profits from the bottled drinks more than made up for that small loss.

One evening when they returned, the water lady was angry. "So, you take my ice and use it to keep your bottle cold and make big money selling. My ice, my water, my box and you are making big money. The other boys told me. Go now! And don't come back. If I see your faces again I will call police!" She pushed them out of her compound and slammed the gate.

"Time to buy one of those boxes," said Modou as they walked away.

"Yes!" exclaimed Umaru, now a staunch supporter of business. "Our own box."

They bought their own Styrofoam cooler and left it at the Mauritanian's store overnight. In the morning they filled it with ice and drinks from his refrigerator, carried them to the beach and sold them. Business prospered.

One morning after they had left the store and passed over the dunes above the shore, Modou stopped. Tucked in among the trees on the slope above the beach was a craft market that catered to tourists.

"They are selling there," he said, "wood carvings and things for tourists."

"Yes, let's go." said Umaru, pulling his sleeve.

Modou continued to eye the market stalls and their displays of wood carvings, baskets and other souvenirs. "It's a long way to come here from the other end of the beach. You know many of those tourists are a little bit fat. They get hot if they walk much. They like to lie still. To come down here is too far for most of them. Let's go and visit those shops a little. Maybe those woodcarvers would like to drink some Coca Cola and talk business."

Thus they added to their inventory postcards and some small woodcarvings they could carry in their pockets. These sold so well they purchased a backpack so Umaru could carry a larger stock of carvings. At first the carvers gave them only the cheaper pieces but as they grew to trust the boys, they consigned more expensive items to them. Their profits increased.

Many of the tourists who bought from them sometimes wondered when they had returned to their homes why they had bought such rough little carvings. But when they remembered the beach under the palms and the boy with the laughing eyes, they smiled and thought the little piece of wood well worth what they had paid.

"Business! Business! Business!" sang Umaru one evening as they made their way through the bush to their house. "Business good for me, Business good for you, Business making rich boys of Modou and Umaru. Business…"

This impromptu melody was abruptly cut off when three figures sprang from the shadows and pinned them to the ground. They struggled and shouted and were punched and kicked until they were silent. The big boys took all the money from their pockets and left them lying in pain.

"Aieee," grunted Modou as he sat up, holding his stomach. Umaru was curled up sobbing. "You OK?"

Umaru crawled over to Modou and leaned against him. "Oh," he sniffed. "You?"

"Just my belly," said Modou. "But all our money is gone."

"Mmm," groaned Umaru, then whispered, "But we still have some hidden in our house."

The following days they varied the route they used to go to their house, never following the same path twice. This strategy seemed to be working, but a week later they returned one evening to find their house thrown over. The bag of money they had buried beneath it was gone.

Stealthily they moved their house to another location and lay down in the darkness. Long after Umaru had gone to sleep, Modou lay awake, thinking.

From: *The West African Intelligencer*

Dazanian Rebels Don't Exist?

By Rick Barry

Government officials in Masongala today heatedly denied reports that rebellious villagers were forming armed groups to resist plundering by the Dazanian National Army.

"These reports are nonsense," said a Ministry of the Interior spokesman. "This rumor of a rebel movement has been concocted by enemies of this government, by enemies of Dazania."

Asked to explain the large-scale movement of troops to the northern parts of the country in response to civil unrest there, the government replied that hooligans and troublemakers were fomenting dissension amongst the simple rural people and the army was deployed to prevent trouble, not to cause it.

Villagers in the north steadfastly declare that there was no trouble until the army arrived and that they armed themselves only after soldiers raided their food stocks.

From: *The West African Intelligencer*

Unlikely Hero
By Rick Barry

Opposition groups in Dazania are unifying under a new symbol. It's called the Toofas Coalition and while government sources deny its existence, the phrase is being murmured everywhere in the streets of the capital city, Masongala.

It's hard to separate legend from reality in this case but the story is that Toofas is the name of a street kid. Apparently police have been unsuccessfully chasing this boy for years, although there are no charges against him. His only crime is his life as a street child. Toofas' legendary escapes and cocky attitude have captured hearts and minds here where the people are suffering daily under ever more repressive police and military abuses of power.

Police in Masongala have reportedly been instructed to shoot the boy on sight but confusion reigns since like other heroes of mythic proportions, there are a dozen different descriptions of him and only a handful of police officers claim to be able to identify him.

Toofas is described as a clever young boy who is fast on his feet and refuses to bow to the might of the police. His escape from them in crowded Manjako Market is fast becoming the stuff of legend. Police apparently had trapped him in the market aisles so he took to the roofs. After making a spectacular leap over the heads of a crowd of cheering onlookers and cursing policemen, he landed on the beach and soon he left his uniformed pursuers far behind.

The Toofas movement appears to be a broad coalition of popular opposition to the current regime. The spirit of this street kid, Toofas, has become the rallying point. Opposition groups, sharing no common political agenda, formerly posed little threat to the Dafo government. Toofas has changed all that. In the streets and markets of Masongala, mere mention of his name brings a smile. President Yusufu Dafo would be well advised to find out why the people are smiling.

Nine

Jason slowed to a halt and bent over with his hands resting on his knees. He had had a good run along Kadanka Road. Behind the tourist hotels it followed the half-moon curve of Kadanka Bay for about ten kilometers. His usual run from Kadanka Point, which marked one end of the bay, to Makalo Point at the other end and then back, made for a thorough workout. The sweat dripped from his forehead and he watched the drops form dark circles when they struck the sandy roadside. His house in Casarica was near the other end of Kadanka Bay and several times each week he jogged the length of the road and back before loping down to the beach for a swim. It was a fine way to end a day.

Now he stood again, stretched and flexed, then began the return leg. Within a hundred meters he had reached the pace and rhythm that made him feel he could run forever. He floated with this until the last half kilometer and then increased his speed for the final sprint. When he reached the pathway that led over the dunes and down to the shore, he dropped into a ragged trot. On the beach, he doffed his backpack, t-shirt and shoes, and waded out to lie on his back in the cool water while his heart rate subsided.

The molten, red-orange sun simmered on the ocean's

golden rim and the lights twinkled on at the outdoor beach bar at the rear of the Makalo Hotel. Suddenly feeling hungry, Jason decided to have his supper there. The fish and chips were excellent, as was the Dazanian-brewed beer, kept very cold for tourists.

As he approached the bar, he noticed a local boy strolling beside the wall that separated the Makalo Hotel grounds from the beach. The boy stopped and looked idly around. Jason squinted. The clothes were different, neat clean shorts and t-shirt instead of rags, but the boy was unmistakably one of the boys who had stolen his money in the market, the one who had signed himself "Modou." The boy's scanning gaze stopped when his eyes met Jason's and his eyes widened. He turned casually then and moved away down the beach. Jason followed him.

"Hey," called Jason. "Stop, I want to talk to you."

"No, thank you." The voice was light with a hint of laughter in it. "I'm too much busy right now."

Jason moved closer and the boy began to trot down toward the flat hard sand on the shore. Jason followed him.

"Stop. I just want to talk to you."

"Just call my secretary." Now the laugh was audible. "Make appointment." The boy increased his pace to a loose jog trot.

"OK, Mr. Modou," muttered Jason to himself as he set a speed to close the gap between them. But the gap did not close. Jason accelerated but each additional burst of momentum that he drew from himself was met by a similar increase from the boy. Finally he was running at the top of his form and still failing to gain. If anything, the distance between them yawned wider with each stride. The boy in front of him seemed to be gliding over the glistening sand, occasionally casting a glance back and flashing a smile. They passed the last of the hotels and the beach was deserted. There was only the soft whisper of the sea and the slap of their feet on the sand. Jason suddenly felt heavy and muscle-bound and realized he was winded, panting like a steam engine. He fell further behind and then gave up and stood watching the boy run. He was not even working. His feet seemed scarcely to touch the sand. He was just playing. Modou looked back over the sixty meters that separated them and grinned. Then he spun into a cartwheel with a laugh of victory and sped away until he was invisible in the deepening twilight.

Jason was irritated as he walked back toward the beach bar. Then the red sunset and the lazy murmur of the waves soothed his ruffled feelings. He smiled ruefully. The boy could run. Jason hated to be beaten but it was a pleasure to see someone run like that.

In his college days Jason had seriously considered a professional career in sports. Gold medals in the state track and field championships proved he had the potential. But he realized in his final year that, as much as he loved running for personal pleasure, he disliked the world of competitive athletics. He had continued to train almost as hard as ever because he liked it. But for his work and creative satisfaction he had combined two of his main interests, travel and journalism, into what he hoped would be a career.

"*Toubab!*" The husky treble voice seemed very close, almost in his ear. He turned. The boy was about ten meters behind him.

"You run fast for a *toubab*."

Jason took a step toward him but the boy skipped away.

"I think," Jason replied, "I think you run better than

any young boy I've ever seen. You're very fast." Then he continued down the beach, determined not to turn back again.

"Your name Jason, yes?"

He judged the boy was about five meters behind. "Yes. And you're Modou."

The giggle that erupted was very close. "How you know my name?"

"You left me a note. Remember?"

"Jason. Here."

Jason stopped and turned. Modou stretched out his arm, something in his hand. Jason reached out and moved toward him until he was close enough to take what was offered. It was a balled-up fifty-kuroma note, the same amount that was stolen from his wallet that day in the market. He flattened its wrinkles and put it into his pocket.

"Why?"

"I'm sorry I tiefed you," the boy said gaily, then added more soberly, "Is not good to tief somebody." They walked side by side now, though Modou kept a safe distance between them.

"Rob," said Jason, "not 'tief.' When you rob somebody, then you are a thief."

"Aha! I'm sorry I rob you." In a lugubrious voice Modou added, "I'm so sorry I'm a thief." They walked in silence for a minute and then he said, "Thank you for that English."

"You're welcome," said Jason, "But I still want to know why."

"I'm not understanding."

"You had a plan in the market and it worked. You think and you plan and then you do something. So, when I say 'why?' I'm asking you what's your plan for me now?"

Modou snickered, "Oh sir, you are very correct." Jason detected a note of reluctant admiration. "But is not a bad plan. This one is a very good plan."

"What?"

"I go tell you later. Now I must look my friend." He reached out and put his hand on Jason's arm. "Where you going?"

Jason moved toward the beach bar tables scattered across the sand, each under a miniature palm thatch and bearing a flickering candle. "There," he said. "If you and your friend are hungry, come and eat with me."

"Fry fish?"

"If you like."

"I am coming," cried Modou as he melted into the darkness.

Five minutes later he reappeared with a smaller boy by his side. They stood uncertainly in the shadows on the opposite side of the table from Jason. "*Jodo-do*!" he said, indicating two chairs opposite himself.

The boys' faces cracked big smiles. "Wonderful!" exclaimed Modou. "You are speaking Fula. I never saw a *toubab* speaking Fula."

"*Jodo-do* – sit down. That's all I know. Maybe you'll teach me some more sometime."

A waiter dressed in a red and white uniform shirt came to their table. He glanced at the boys then looked at Jason. There was something a little cynical in his gaze.

"These boys are bothering you?" asked the waiter.

"No. Not at all. I invited them to eat with me."

"Only that sometimes these boys on the beach force themselves on tourists."

"No, it's Ok. I know them from somewhere else."

Modou grinned and looked down at the table. Jason ordered fish and chips for all, soft drinks for the boys and beer for himself.

"So, you're on holiday from your work at the market?" he said when the waiter had brought their drinks.

"No. We working here now," said Modou

"Things got too hot for you at the market?"

"No, but is too many roundups."

"What's that?"

"Oh, roundups is when police, many police, come into the market and take all street boys for jail."

"For robbing?" asked Jason.

"No, is not necessary to rob. Any boy in Manjako they go collect for jail. They like to just take everyone," said Modou.

"And then what happens, when you are in the jail?"

"They wait small, maybe you are having rich friend or big brother who go come and give them some money for let you go. After, they take every boys out and load for inside one truck. They drive truck far far, push all boys out, beat them small: Pung! Pung! Pung! And leave them."

"So that's why you're here?"

"Oh, is not just that. Is not enough money for market. Is OK for eat and there is small work, but not enough. Is all Africans there and they are not having no money."

"And there is more money here on the beach?"

"Oh yes. Many rich *toubab* tourists here," said Modou.

"You're looking very well dressed now."

"By force! Tourists don't like to be seeing dirty old clothes and if tourist police see we are wearing old raggedy thing, they go chase we." Modou grinned. "But we are liking to be wearing nice clothes."

"So why were you wearing rags like when I saw you in the market?" asked Jason

"Oh, in Manjako we are begging many times. Nobody go give we anything if we are looking like rich boy. We must be dirty and miserable for make money begging."

"That must be hard work."

"Oh, no, dirty is very easy. When you living in market, is hard work to be clean. But dirty is not hard work." Modou shook his head.

"And miserable?"

Modou laughed. "Oh sir, is very hard to be miserable. But we trying."

"Modou, how old are you?"

"Eighteen," said Modou.

Jason laughed. "Modou, if you're a day over eleven I'd be surprised."

"Sixteen," said Modou.

"Ok. I'll give you twelve, last offer."

"Fourteen, sir, I think. Is only me to count and I never know for long time when one year is finish and next year is start."

"OK, fourteen." Jason turned to the other boy. "You, I don't even know your name."

"Umaru."

"OK, Umaru, how old are you?"

Umaru giggled. "Sixteen!" He blushed.

"What do you think, Modou? Is Umaru sixteen?"

"He like to be sixteen." Modou looked at Umaru with a fond measuring expression. "But I'm thinking he is more young than me, small, maybe eleven or twelve."

The fish and chips arrived and they all concentrated on satisfying their appetites.

When they had cleaned their plates both boys politely thanked him and accepted his offer of another soft drink.

"OK, so there are lots of rich tourists on the beach. But how do you get their money?" asked Jason.

"We are selling."

"Selling what?" Jason watched as Modou made circles on the tablecloth with his forefinger. "Ganja?"

"Oh, no. Is one bad business. Many bad peoples are doing that. Is not for small boys like we. We are selling cold drink and wood carving, like mask and statue, souvenir of Dazania."

"Where are they?"

"Oh, we not have any now. When it is day we collect them from carvers and carry them down beach until we are seeing tourists. You, Jason, you are teacher?"

"No, I'm a journalist."

"Journalist?"

"A writer. I write stories for the newspaper. What made you think I was a teacher?"

"You look like teacher. Your face look like is thinking very hard," said Modou. "But you running too fast for teacher."

"And you, now that you're making lots of money here on the beach, what do you plan to do with it?"

Modou looked up from beneath lowered brows. "Ah. I go tell you sometime. You are living here, yes?"

"Yes, not far from here, in Casarica."

"And you are coming for beach every day?"

"Not every day, but three or four times a week."

"And how long you go stay for this Dazania?"

"I don't know. Maybe for a long time, one or two years maybe."

"Ah huh," grunted Modou. He pondered this information for a minute then looked at Umaru. The smaller boy met his gaze for a few seconds. Then Modou turned to Jason. "You see, we are having a problem."

"Yes?"

"Is too many bad people here on beach for night. And sometimes when we are sleeping they go come for tief we, rob we."

"Where do you sleep?"

Modou gestured toward a bushy, forested area beyond the hotel grounds. "There."

"And they take your money?"

"Yes. Is very hard to collect any money because they go come and take it just anytime. You see, this life for market or for beach is not good for long time. You just go on same same. Maybe we are wanting to be making a little business or something, but it go take many big money. When big boys are just robbing, robbing, robbing we, all we ever go have is small money."

"But you have no family to help you? I thought everyone in this country had family."

"Only small family," the boy said, sober for an instant. Then he looked up at Jason. "I got Umaru." He glanced at the other boy. "And Umaru, he got me."

"I see," said Jason. He suddenly felt isolated and alone, and a little envious.

"So we are wanting our money to big," said Modou, resuming his business tone, "but when we are having small money, bad big boys go come every time and take it. If we go to hide it they go follow we and rob it. If we keep it on our bodies they go beat we for take it. In daytime they are hiding so tourist police is not seeing them, but all nights, they go hunt for beach."

"Why don't you go somewhere else at night?"

"They follow we and when is dark they go take our money."

"What can you do?" asked Jason.

"We are thinking maybe we go find somebody take care for our money," said Modou, fixing Jason with his eyes. Jason chuckled and Modou continued, "...somebody who come for beach every time...." Jason burst out laughing. Modou, undaunted by Jason's laughter, persevered, "... somebody who live close for beach, one good somebody, then our money go get big."

"So this is your plan. I see."

"Is a good plan, isn't it?" asked Modou with a satisfied air.

"OK," laughed Jason. "How do we do it?"

"You go keep one small notebook. When we are giving money you go write in book so you are knowing how much is for we. When we have enough, we go come and collect how much we are needing and you go minus it for book."

"You have one small notebook?" asked Jason.

"No, but you are having one. In that your pack." Modou spoke more loudly to pierce through Jason's laughter. "Oh yes, I must tell you! Is not good for leave your pack like that on beach and go swimming. You know, anyone can just be coming and be looking inside, collecting any nice thing they are seeing inside..."

"You're a very dangerous boy!" said Jason. He paused. "That fifty-kuroma bill?"

"You are just leaving money lying loose for open pack like that." Modou shrugged his shoulders helplessly. "You not even knowing money is gone, is true isn't it?"

"Well, no," admitted Jason. "But how am I ever to trust you? Really, every time I turn around you're robbing me."

"You go trust me, Jason, because I go trust you." Modou pulled some bills from his pocket, separated a fifty-kuroma note and offered it to Jason. "First, here is your own fifty kuromas from market long time back. Now is finish. Yes?"

"OK."

Modou offered a second fifty-kuroma note.

"And what's this?" asked Jason.

"Management fee."

Jason snorted.

"You see, I am taking one fifty kuromas for pay you back for Manjako fifty. And then I am thinking, well, say plan no go work? I must be having something for my trouble…"

"Oh," said Jason with some difficulty. "Plan B."

"What is that Plan B?"

"When you have a plan, that's Plan A. If Plan A doesn't work, you should have another plan ready. That other plan, for when something goes wrong, that's what we call Plan B."

"Aha! So, Plan A is going along fine fine. No need for Plan B. Take fifty kuromas. And here is our first money for put in book, two hundred kuromas."

"This is not from robbing? I won't keep money from robbing."

"No, no. Is good money. Truly! I'm not robbing normally. Only you."

"Only me?"

"Oh yes! You are thinking I robbing every peoples? No. I looking very carefully. Not just any somebody, you know. Must be very special somebody."

Jason giggled. "I'll always remember this as my nicest robbery. Very excellent."

"We are trying, sir."

Jason rummaged around in his pack for the notebook.

He opened it to a blank page and wrote, "Modou and Umaru—Accounts." Then he wrote down the amount of their deposit and sat back and looked at them.

Modou's boyishly handsome face was full of mischief and could be moved by its owner to a hundred expressions. When Jason looked at him, what he saw was appealing, but he felt that he was seeing only the surface. Yet that was part of Modou's charm. What you saw was sweet and funny and it suggested that what you were not allowed to see was even better. Umaru's face shone with innocence, no subterfuge or hidden depths there, a sweetness, an openness and a vulnerability almost embarrassing.

"I think Umaru is a bad liar," said Jason with a smile.

Modou laughed, "Oh, Umaru one useless boy for lie. I am trying to teach him but he just not understand how to be lying."

Umaru wriggled and blushed under their combined gaze.

Jason met Modou's eyes across the table and he held out his hand. "This is going to be very interesting, Modou. Thank you."

Modou shook his hand gravely. "You're welcome, Jason." His eyes twinkled. "I am thinking maybe you are a little bit dangerous, too." Then he turned to Umaru. "Let us go now and be finding our place for sleeping."

They stood, both thanked him and shook his hand again and then were gone into the night.

Jason ordered another beer and tried to remember when he had last giggled—not since he was fourteen. He laughed again when he reviewed the evening. He had been beaten in a race, robbed, conned and manipulated, and he had not had so much fun in months. He decided to credit their account with the fifty kuroma 'management fee.' The kid had earned it. The night wind swept in from the Atlantic and he listened to it moaning in the black trees beyond the hotel.

A few weeks later, jogging up to his starting point on Kadanka Road, Jason saw Modou and Umaru, squatting under a mango tree, obviously waiting for him. Since his first meeting with them on the beach they had found him a half dozen times. Each time they had made a deposit and he had noted it in the book.

"Jason," called Modou as he came up to them. "Today I'm running with you. OK?"

"Yes, fine," he answered as he shook hands with them.

"But, you know, running on road is not good. To be running with naked feet on beach is best."

"We say 'bare feet,' not 'naked feet.'"

"OK. Bare feet is best. Thank you for English."

They walked through the forest and over the dunes to the beach. Jason left his shoes and pack with Umaru and he and Modou ran down to the firm wet sand where the waves foamed and sparkled on the shore.

After they had jogged for a little while, side by side, Jason asked Modou to run in front of him.

"You want I beat you?" smiled Modou.

"No I just want you to run in front of me so I can look at your style."

After a hundred meters he called Modou to slow down and run beside him. "OK, now let's let it out a little."

"More fast?"

"Yes, faster, but just stay a little ahead of me."

As they flew down the beach Jason noted carefully the angle of Modou's arms, the set of his shoulders, the lift of his heels and knees, the rhythm of his breathing and the tilt of his head and torso.

After a kilometer he shouted, "OK Modou, let it all out. Go!"

The transformation was amazing, like some hidden source of energy surged into the lean muscles and fired the legs into a blur of motion. He left Jason like he was standing still.

"Jesus!" muttered Jason. "Fourteen years old."

He let him race two hundred meters then megaphoned his hands and shouted, "OK. Come back."

Jason led them through a set of stretches and calisthenics until they had cooled down. Then they sat on the sand.

"How long have you been running?" asked Jason.

"Always," said Modou. "Even when I small small boy I remember standing still is sometimes too hard and I just run. Then I am feeling free. I am wanting it to be going on forever. And sometimes, you know, I need to run, maybe I am chasing something." A gurgle of laughter escaped him. "Or maybe somebody is chasing me."

"You could run faster. You could run better," said Jason.

"You go show me, please sir."

"We can try. Do you run every day?"

"Yes."

"What about Umaru? Doesn't he like to run?"

"Oh no, he say he has only small running in him and he like to be saving it for dangerous. He like to be singing so when I'm running he go sit for beach making his small songs."

"He makes his own songs?"

"Oh yes! Anything we are doing he is singing it. You know his heart is very sweet and even when he is talking sometimes, is like a kind of singing." He paused. "Now tell me how I go run faster."

"OK. Listen carefully. From the waist down your style is naturally almost perfect. But above the waist you're a mess. Arms flying all over the place, head flopping about like a coconut on a string. Right now you're only running with your legs. When you learn to run with your whole body you'll run much faster and easier. Today we'll start with your arms." Then Jason showed him how he could balance his body weight more evenly by moving his arms alternately in time with his legs, how to stretch and bend them to make the perfect counterpoints to his leg movements.

Modou practiced while they jogged further down the beach, then they broke into a slow lope until he had the rhythm working for him.

"Aha!" grunted Jason, "You feel it now, don't you."

"Jason," called Modou, looking back with a delirious smile, "I am sorry. I must run now."

Jason watched again as the transformation took place and said to himself, "He just pushes some button and bingo! Suddenly he's going twice as fast."

When they came back to where Umaru waited they went through another set of cool down exercises, then swam until they were refreshed. Jason lolled on his back while the two boys splashed and laughed.

They dressed and the boys proffered another deposit. Jason updated the account book.

"Sir," said Umaru.

Jason looked up, surprised. Modou usually did all the talking. Modou was grinning, his eyes sliding back and forth between Umaru and Jason. Umaru was standing stiffly at attention.

"Yes, Umaru?" Jason resisted the temptation to add, "at ease, soldier."

"You are very good," he said and began to melt into a blush. Modou elbowed him. "And we want to eat you!" finished Umaru breaking into a big smile.

"Eat with you," shot Modou out of the side of his mouth. "With you!"

"With you. Eat with you," stated Umaru with another triumphant smile.

"We are paying everything," said Modou. "Even beer. Is bad for you, you know. Drinking alcohol is very bad. But you are not Muslim so maybe is OK. You going for hell anyway. Please?"

"Fry fish?" choked Jason

"If yah like," responded Modou in a nearly American accent.

From: *The Masongala Daily Banner*

Street Vendors to be Licensed?
By Jason Andrews

"Many cities in other parts of the world are increasing their revenues by this means," stated Mayor of Masongala, Ousman Ceesay, at a recent meeting of the Masongala City Council. "In addition, licensing provides a means of control over vendors that will allow us to determine where vendors can operate and what kinds of marketing practices are acceptable," he said.

City councilors are concerned about the recent proliferation of street vendors and their makeshift stalls in the streets of the capital. "These stalls and street salesmen are just congesting our already busy streets," said one councilor.

Another councilor noted that, "Street vendors simply take business away from established businesses that have invested a great deal in their stores, only to find they are being outsold by people standing right on their doorsteps."

National Police Force of Dazania Masongala City Liaison Officer, Sub-Inspector Ebu Ndiaye, said he welcomed the proposal. "Up to now there is little we can do to control street vendors. The congestion they cause is often used by criminals to steal from passersby and to evade police. Vendors often sell stolen merchandise and thieves may disguise themselves as vendors in order to pass unnoticed in the crowds."

MCC Social Welfare Officer, Mariama Dom, drew councilors' attention to the problem with children vending and said she had been discussing this issue with Rights for Kids Coalition, an international NGO dedicated to establishing children's rights in Dazania. "One of the things we should be looking at is an acceptable age for vendors," she said. "There are many children selling sweets and cigarettes in the streets who should be attending school."

From: *The West African Intelligencer*

Dazania Destination for Sex Tourists?
By Rick Barry

Tourists visiting the sunny African shores of Dazania are not just looking for a good tan claims a recent report by Sexploitation Watch, an international NGO that monitors the sexual exploitation of women and children. The report states, "There is a large scale industry in Dazania that caters to the sexual needs of tourists."

The report describes websites devoted to discussion of how and where to obtain sex in Dazania and says that both male and female travelers exploit Dazanians sexually during their vacations and travel to Dazania specifically for that purpose.

In a communiqué addressed to the government of Dazania, Sexploitation Watch called for "legislation to protect the women and children of Dazania from this world-wide scourge," and demanded that tour operators openly catering to sex tourists be delicensed and perpetrators of crimes against women and children be severely punished.

From: *The Masongala Daily Banner*

NPFD and RKC Join to Fight Sex Tourism
By Jason Andrews

The National Police Force of Dazania today announced the commencement of a joint effort with the Rights for Kids Coalition to examine the sex tourism industry in Dazania. An NPFD spokesman said the police were very concerned about recent reports of visitors to Dazania taking advantage of women and children provided for them in bars and on the beaches. "Perpetrators of these heinous crimes will be seriously prosecuted," said the spokesman.

RKC Country Program Director Reba Brecken said that Dazania was becoming a notorious destination for sex tourists, particularly those interested in sex with juveniles. "This is a clear violation of the rights of children," she stated, "and we welcome the opportunity to work with the NPFD to put a stop to this traffic."

NPFD will form and train special investigation and tactical squads to deal with the problem. Initial funding of $50,000 for the program has been approved by RKC.

Ten

Jason saved the article he was composing and went to answer a knock on his door. It was Modou and Umaru, wearing shy grins. Umaru balanced on his head a large plastic bag full of clothes.

"Modou and Umaru! Welcome!"

"Good afternoon, sir," said Modou formally. Umaru just smiled. "We are not seeing you for beach. Is two days now and we are having too much money."

"I'm sorry. I've been busy lately," he said and invited them into the house. They looked around.

"Oooo!" said Modou. "Look this house! Jason you are having one very nice house."

"I like it. Come, I'll show you around." He led them through the parlor into the kitchen and then to the large bathroom and combined laundry area, and the three bedrooms. They marveled at his fridge and stove and demanded a long explanation of how the toilet worked. They thought it a strange and amusing device.

"Sir, I have one question," said Modou as they stood in the spare bedroom that Jason used as a home office. "Where you keep our money?"

Jason moved to the desk, extracted a key from the

center drawer and unlocked one of the side drawers. He pulled out a large envelope and showed them the money inside.

"You know, it's getting to be a lot of money. I've been thinking that maybe I should be keeping it in the bank," said Jason.

"No sir, please," said Modou. We are liking to have it here. Bank is sometimes open, sometimes close. You want your money? Bank is close, you are crying. Here is our money we have for you today."

Jason noted on the envelope how much they gave him, put it back in the drawer and locked it.

"You are having one maid?"

"Yes, there's a woman who comes in some mornings to do the laundry and clean up."

"Then let us be hiding this in a better place," said Modou taking the key and looking around the room. He was finally satisfied to put it on the lintel above the door.

"What's in the bag?" asked Jason when they had returned to the parlor.

"Sir, is our dirty clothes. We are thinking you are having water and we must come to see you so…"

"You want to wash your clothes?"

"Yes, sir."

Jason took them into the bathroom and showed them the laundry tubs and soap. Then he went back to his laptop and the article he was composing. He was not used to having other people in his house but the happy chatter coming from the bathroom was only a brief distraction and he was soon engrossed once again in his writing.

An hour had passed when Modou poked his head around the door. "Jason?"

"Yes?"

"Can we be washing our bodies? With hot water and soap? In your bathtub?"

"You have no bathtub in your house?" said Jason.

"Oh yes! We are having one big bathtub. Is bigger than your small bathtub, you know, very big water with small salt inside," said Modou. "But is no hot water. Peoples are saying hot water is very nice for bath."

"It is. But it's very hot. You can even burn yourself." In the bathroom he put the plug in the tub and turned on both taps, showing them how to mix the hot and cold until the temperature was comfortable. He reached for towels and bath soap and when he turned back, both boys were standing unselfconsciously naked beside the tub. He returned to his desk and for another hour a happy murmur interspersed with squeals and ripples of laughter provided a pleasant background to his work.

When he put his head inside the bathroom door, both boys were chest deep in suds and laughing. "Jason!" said Modou. "Bath is very nice. We are enjoying."

"I can see that. Look, I am going to make some food. Would you like to eat with me?"

"Fry fish?"

"No. But I have some cold chicken and some bread and other things."

"Chicken is good!" said Modou.

"We can stay for bathtub?" asked Umaru.

"I'll call you when it's time to eat."

Fifteen minutes later he had laid out the food and set the table. When he went into the bathroom they were still in the tub. He pulled the plug, drew the shower curtain and told them to stand up. Then he ran the taps until the mix was right and pulled the plunger that activated the shower. "This will wash all the soap and dirty water off," he explained. The shower delighted them as much as the bath and he had to call them again before he heard the taps being shut off.

The boys' clothes were damp from their splashing in the bathroom so they both came into the dining area wearing towels. While they ate, Modou and Jason talked about running. They had been training together now for several weeks and Modou's style was greatly improved. Jason had clocked Modou at various distances and found that the boy performed better at shorter distances, not surprisingly, since at his age he did not have the stamina for more sustained trials. Puberty and its potential for increased muscle mass was only just arriving. He had made a videotape of the boy running, in order to further an idea that had begun to simmer in the back of his mind.

When the chicken had been reduced to a few bones that the boys were crunching between their strong, white teeth, Jason said, "When we first met you said you would tell me sometime what you plan to do with all your money."

"Yes," answered Modou. "I go tell you. But sir, please, you are not telling any peoples about our plan or about our money?"

"I promise. I won't tell anybody."

"You go laugh," said Modou suspiciously.

"No. I promise I won't laugh."

"Sir, we are wanting to go for school. The money is for rent one small room and pay our school fees and for buying food when we are going to school. Also, for uniforms and books."

"You need so much?"

"Yes, is too cost to go for school. We want to

be having enough for us to school one full year, just studying, no working. We are not having enough now, but soon soon. Maybe two more months if business is good."

"You want to go to school."

"Yes. Is not good to be poor like we. We are wanting to be somebodies."

Both boys looked earnestly at him over the table. Jason was speechless.

"Jason?" said Modou.

Jason raised his eyebrows.

"You are thinking we are foolish small boys?"

"No. I'm thinking, you don't know it, but you're somebodies already. I think it's a wonderful plan and I'm happy, I'm proud to be able to help any way that I can."

"You are like our plan?" squirmed Umaru, beaming.

"Yes. It's a very good plan," said Jason. "But what kind of somebody do you want to be? What do you want to do when you have some education?"

Modou laughed, "Umaru say he like to be a counter."

"A counter?"

"Yes, is sweet."

"What's a counter?"

"Oh, is when they count you, count the boys in the street," said Modou. "You know, is one person having some papers and nice small suitcase, good pen. They going to ask you so many questions. Where you from? What you doing? What you eating? Where you sleeping? You eating any drug? They like to be asking about sexing. You doing any sexing? Who you sexing? Got any problem with penis?" Modou laughed. "I am saying, 'Is no problem with penis. He working fine fine. Stomach is problem.' They go write all then they give you small money or sometimes buy some food."

"Someone doing a survey, I guess."

"Yes, sometimes they say is survey. Three times when we living for market different peoples are coming for count we. Umaru say it nice work like that, talking to children, asking them so many questions and then giving them small money or food. He like that big car and nice pen."

"What do you want to do?"

"Maybe business man. I don't know. Education first, then working. I like to be in office maybe. Nice clothes, having one small TV on your table..."

"Computer."

"Yes, playing computer and talking to the peoples who are coming. You want to see me? Make appointment with my one beautiful girl for secretary. She is sitting there with big breasts, nice long hairs. I go see you next week. Is good. With education you can do so many things. Maybe I will be journalist! Is nice work, telling the peoples what is happening."

Jason's mind flashed to the unfinished story still sitting on his desktop. It would be midnight before he would be able to do the final editing. Umaru said something to Modou in Fula. Modou nodded.

"What did he say?" asked Jason.

"He say you thinking about your work you are doing and we small boys are troubling you. He say we should go to our house now."

"He's right. I do have work to do. But you small boys don't trouble me. I've enjoyed your visit and I hope you'll come again."

"Thank you, sir," they said in unison.

From: *The Masongala Daily Banner*

RKC Lauds Licensing of Vendors
By Jason Andrews

Masongala City Council's recent decision to license street vendors was hailed by Rights for Kids Coalition Country Program
Director Reba Brecken as "a step in the right direction." Noting
that age of vendors would be a primary criterion in assessing suit-
ability for licensing, Ms. Brecken said, "We are happy that the
MCC has accepted our recommendation that the minimum age
for a street vendor license be set at eighteen years of age. This
will comply with RKC guidelines and encourage parents to send
their children to school instead of trying to make money off their
labors in the streets."

Responding to parents' complaints in the media that they
could only afford to send children to school if the children earned
a portion of their fees by vending in their spare time, Ms. Brecken
stated, "Parents must recognize that the education of their children is the responsibility of parents and that children should not
be expected to contribute to the costs of their education."

From: *The West African Intelligencer*

Kuroma Crumbles
By Rick Barry

In Dazania, the price of rice has risen by 300% in the last year. Rampant inflation has been the most noticeable result of the government's ineffective foreign exchange and currency control policies. The value of the kuroma has declined dramatically since it was allowed to float free on the international market.

Recent scandals regarding government deals with all-inclusive tour operators are another result of the fall in the value of the kuroma. High government officials have apparently been making sweetheart deals with hotel developers whereby foreign currency earned from tourism in Dazania never enters the country, but is paid directly into overseas bank accounts. Many of these overseas accounts are held by officials in the government of Yusufu Dafo. Economists critical of the practice point out that although Dazania shows gross tourism revenues of almost $200M, less than $15M actually enters the country.

While government officials may be finding a windfall in the collapse of the kuroma, the common people of the country are being told to tighten their belts. "Government has been subsidizing the value of the kuroma for a long time," said a Dazania Central Bank spokesman.

"The Dazanian people must realize that we simply have to work harder and produce more if we want the kuroma to return to its former value."

The poorest part of the country, the rural north, has been hardest hit by the rise in the cost of basic foodstuffs. Rumors of food-based riots in several northern towns are rife in the streets of the nation's capital, Masongala. In an ominous response to the suggestion that the government is losing control of the country, an unnamed Dazanian Armed Forces source said that the army was "monitoring the situation closely and would never allow the country to fall into chaos and disorder."

Government officials meanwhile denied there was any dissatisfaction in northern towns and maintained the rumors were being spread by troublemakers such as the mysterious Toofas Coalition, an underground popular movement.

Coach Dan Brown,
Millbank College,
2662 Aspen Avenue,
Millbank, Minnesota

Dear Dan,

You will probably be surprised to be getting such a long letter from me. When you read what I have to say you will be even more surprised.

As you know, I've been living in Africa for nearly ten months now, working for a local paper here in Dazania and selling stories to international news magazines whenever anything interesting happens in this sleepy little country.

I've continued to run and train just for the love of it and that's how I made an exciting discovery. One day, running on the beach I found myself running against a local kid. We started competing as we ran and he played with me a bit. Then he just walked away from me.

Of course, I'm not in as good shape as I was when I ran for Millbank, but my times are only a shade off what they used to be. I was running as fast as I've ever run and this kid just moved away like he was turbocharged.

We've both watched international class athletes perform and you've trained some yourself but I am telling you that you've never seen anything like the way this kid can move. I've clocked him several times now at various distances and you can see for yourself on the attached sheet how fast his times are.

If I'm not mistaken, his time for the 100 meter dash is less than one-tenth of a second off the world record for his age group and his times for other distances could put state and even national trophies in his hands right now, without any further training. The enclosed video (shot last week) will give you an idea of his speed and style, though it's not his fastest time or his smoothest run.

You'll be even more surprised when I tell you that this kid is only fourteen and that he's a street kid with no training other than a few tips from me. He doesn't even go to school and makes his living selling souvenirs to tourists. He's an orphan and lives in a cardboard box in the bush near the beach.

Best of all, this boy has what you used to tell us was most important in a runner. He's got heart. When he runs he gives it everything. In fact, sometimes I'm scared by how totally he gives himself. It seems almost dangerous and I always find myself with my heart in my throat when I tell him to go, to give it all he's got. He loves to run and has no idea of just how good he is. He's every track coach's dream come true, a once in a lifetime athlete.

OK, I can already hear you planning how to get him over there where he can be properly looked after and trained. How do we make this happen? The main problem is money. I'll handle all the paperwork, etc. on this side but I can't contribute anything financially – I like what I do but it doesn't pay enough to afford anything beyond a reasonably comfortable life in this backwater. I'm still paying off my student loans and am real pleased when I can get through the month without an overdraft.

What I need to hear from you is that you can arrange all travel costs, a full scholarship at a local junior secondary school, living expenses, and that you are prepared to act as guardian. He's had a bit of education and with a good tutor can probably catch up to his age group in a year or two.

One other thing I know you will worry about, his psychological fitness. Can he cope with all the change, can he cope with the pressures of competition? The boy is really intelligent, well balanced, nice and funny. In fact, he's a real pleasure to be around. Not the slightest hint of prima donna neurosis. I expect he would be completely cool and focused in competition. He's amazingly confident and self-contained.

I've not said anything to the boy, Modou, about any of this yet since I want to have something solid in place before I tell him. It would be very cruel to build up his hopes and then have to disappoint him.

I know this is a big commitment I am asking you to make but when you see this kid really run, even once, you will feel it's all worthwhile. Let me know whatever other information you need from me. Give me a call if you want— my number is ------. The country code is ---.

I look forward to hearing from you soon.

Yours truly,
Jason Andrews

Eleven

Modou and Umaru were stopped by the tourist police in the late afternoon. Business had been good that day but their remaining stock and the day's take were confiscated. The officers harassed them for selling without a license. When they asked how to get a license the police told them it was impossible since they were underage. They warned the boys not to be caught selling again.

"Aieee," groaned Modou as they scuffed down the beach. "These policemen are very wicked to be taking all our money. Nothing now even to be buying food. It's too bad."

"Well," reflected Umaru, "at least they didn't beat us."

"Yes, that's true. But what are we going to do?"

"Maybe we can go live in the market again," offered Umaru.

"No. Market is finished. It's not like before. Now the police are doing roundups every week. If they see us they're going to pick us up, anytime at all. Roundup is very bad, too."

They walked in silence for a few minutes. Umaru put his arm around Modou's waist and said, "It's a nice day. Sun is shining. I am walking on the beach with my friend. Life is very sweet."

"You're a very foolish boy," said Modou as he draped his arm around Umaru's shoulder. "Very foolish boy."

"It's no problem for me to be foolish," said Umaru, "I'm having one friend who is a little bit smart."

"You're like me—it's OK for me to be bad since I'm having one friend who is a little bit good."

"We are very blessed to be having such good friends," said Umaru, "But I think I'm more blessed than you. My friend is very wonderful, the best friend in the world."

"Sorry, Umaru, you are very incorrect. My friend is the best friend in the world," said Modou. "But I have no mind for argument now. I am too starving." He turned them toward the path that led over the dunes to Kadanka Road. "Come, foolish boy, let's go visit Jason and take a little of our money. When my stomach has some nice food to be chewing on then it will leave my head to think about our problem."

Jason was not at home. He was out celebrating. Earlier in the afternoon he had received a telephone call from his editor at *The West African Intelligencer* telling him that his Toofas story had been picked up by international news wire services. It was his first breakthrough into the international press and he felt he deserved a night on the town to celebrate. Not only had the wire services distributed his Toofas story widely but they were asking for more. If he could track this Toofas kid down, fame and fortune beckoned.

That the Toofas story had been printed under his byline pseudonym of Rick Barry did not worry him. He had been advised that when one wanted to cover local news critically while living in a third world country, it was always wise to use a pen name to avoid unwelcome attention from governments sensitive to journalists pointing out their corrupt or inept practices. In Dazanian papers he wrote innocuous articles under his own name. When he wrote for international publications he used his pen name.

It was late when he finally arrived back at his house. Someone moved out of the shadows near his gate.

"Jason," said Modou.

"Modou? Is that you?"

"Yes, just one minute please." He leaned into the shadows and shook Umaru awake. Umaru stumbled sleepily beside them as they walked toward the front door of Jason's house.

"What are you doing here this late? It's nearly one o'clock in the morning."

Modou told him that they needed some of their money. A half hour later the boys were finishing off some fried eggs and bread and two large cups of milky coffee. Jason had given Modou the money he wanted. While they ate, Modou described how they were prohibited from selling on the beach by the new bylaw requiring licenses for street vendors.

As Jason listened he began to formulate a news story about this downside of licensing. But while he was mulling over this possibility it occurred to him that he might have a good source of information about Toofas right in his kitchen. "Modou," he said, interrupting the boy's account of the afternoon's event on the beach, "you used to work in the market. There is one boy there that the police are always looking for, a boy called Toofas. They say the army are looking for him now too and I'd like to talk to him also."

"You want to talk to Toofas?" asked Modou.

"Yes, do you know him? Have you ever met him?"

"Oh, I am thinking Toofas is very hard to find," laughed

- 174 -

Modou. "Maybe even he is just gone." He stood up and walked over to the kitchen window.

"Well, the police can't find him and they sure are looking hard," said Jason. "Do you know where he is?"

"Why you want to be talking to Toofas?" asked Modou, peering out into the night. Then he turned to look at Jason and grinned, "You are not liking to talk to me?"

"No, I like talking to you, but this Toofas, well it's a professional thing. You wouldn't understand."

"Ahuh," grunted Modou and turned back to the window. "OK. Maybe this Toofas is for market. You should be going to Manjako Market and asking the peoples there."

"Yes, I guess that's what I'll have to do."

Modou still seemed quite awake but Umaru was nodding off and toppling from side to side. Modou came back from the window and nudged him. "Sir," he said, dragging Umaru to his feet, "We will be going now."

"My God!" said Jason. "It's two o'clock in the morning. I can't let you go wandering off at this time of night. You can sleep in the guest room."

"Good idea," said Modou. "Bad peoples are chasing us at night. Is very difficult."

Jason gave them some sheets for the bed in his spare bedroom and twenty minutes later the house was asleep.

Two days later the boys were dawdling along the beach at the end where the hotels were smaller and older and began to peter out into the undeveloped stretch of coastline. They often went to that deserted shoreline when they wanted to wash their clothes and bathe. As they passed a small beach bar a tourist called them over to him. It was a young man they had sold some postcards to during the preceding week. He wanted to buy another postcard. He was disappointed they had nothing to sell. They explained that they were no longer allowed to sell on the beach or the tourist police would beat them. The young man proposed a solution. He said he wanted to buy some postcards and maybe some small carvings. If Modou would bring these to him at his hotel after dark when the tourist police had left the beach he would buy some.

"This is very sweet," said Modou as they walked back up the beach to the end where the carvers and souvenir sellers had their shops.

"Yes," said Umaru. "He is a good man. His eyes are smiling nice."

Just before sunset Modou and Umaru parted. "You stay here," said Modou. "There is no need for both of us to be beaten if any bad policemen are around. And I am running faster than you. OK?" Umaru settled down by the Makalo Beach Hotel wall to wait and Modou trotted away, his pockets full of postcards and small carvings.

Two hours later he returned, squatted down beside Umaru and laughed.

"You are laughing," said Umaru.

Modou reached into his pocket and pulled out one hundred kuromas. "I will tell you," he said. "No problem on the beach. The man is having one small house in the Kadanka Court Hotel compound. He is calling it a cabana. It's very nice, bathroom is there, kitchen is there, and one room with bed and tv and nice chairs. So we are talking and I am showing him all the things and he is looking at them. We are sitting on the bed and talking very nice and he is putting his hand on my leg, like so." Modou caressed the inside of Umaru's thigh. "So we are talking about the postcards and he is rubbing my leg a little, like so. Now you know what my penis is like, always standing up all the time."

Umaru snickered, "Penis has no sense. Always wanting to play."

"So my penis is making a bump in my shorts and I am talking postcards and the man is rubbing my leg. Then I am looking in his eyes and I am seeing he is one so very lonely man. He is looking so sad. I am thinking. What? It's a surprise for me, you know, big man wanting to play. So I am leaning against him a little and soon clothes are on the floor and we are lying on the bed having sweet play. After a little while we finish and are lying nice and quiet, feeling good. He is saying it is very wonderful for him. I am one beautiful boy."

"Is nice play?" said Umaru.

"Sexing girl is best, you know, but the man is very nice," said Modou. "He is doing some things…" He laughed. "I will show you later."

Umaru snorted.

"So then I am having nice hot water shower…"

"Yes," said Umaru, sniffing, "I am smelling perfume soap."

"…and then I am getting dressed again and he is giving me this one hundred kuromas. I am asking what postcards he wants to buy. He is laughing and saying he is only taking maybe one postcard now. But he is very happy and he wants to pay me one hundred kuromas for this one postcard."

"One hundred kuromas! For one postcard! Your penis is selling postcards. Good salesman!"

"Now here is the good part. When I am leaving he is saying he wants to buy one postcard tomorrow night too, one from me. And, he is also wanting to buy one postcard from you. If you like to bring one postcard he wants to buy it."

"Do you think he will be paying one hundred kuromas for my one postcard, too?"

"Well, maybe fifty kuromas. You know, it's a smaller postcard, not so big as mine. And I am one beautiful boy, of course."

"He is a good man?"

"Yes, I am thinking he is a good man, but too lonely. Like you are saying, it's hard to have no friend."

"I will bring my postcard!"

"Businessman!" said Modou. "Now let us find some food. I'm too hungry."

The postcard business was lucrative though sporadic. Their first customer finished his holiday but other lonely men who were interested in their postcards by night service arrived from time to time. The boys found they could also make a little money as guides taking tourists to the zoo or the market and protecting them from con artists and pickpockets. They made regular deposits with Jason and their savings began to mount once again. When Jason asked how they were earning money the boys explained they now worked as tourist guides.

One night the boys lay in their house talking. "You know," said Umaru, picking at a shred of cardboard that was dangling above his head. "Sometimes this work is OK. We are eating and making money, but mostly it is not good."

"Nobody is doing anything bad to you. You can always just walk out if you don't like it."

"I know but it still feels wrong to be taking money for sexing."

"You can do it for free if you like," said Modou.

"You know what I mean," said Umaru.

"Yes, but I don't want to think about it. Listen, it's just play," said Modou. "Everybody does it. Either you do it your ownself here or you do it with someone else in Kadanka Court Hotel. Only difference is that if you let someone else do it you get paid for it."

"Yes, but sometimes it feels like lying," Umaru persisted. "When it's over, sometimes I wish I didn't do it. It's hard to understand. Anyway, it makes me to be thinking."

"Mmm?"

"That man tonight now, that Mr. James, do you think what he was saying is good?"

"He wanting us to stay with him in his house all the time?"

"Yes, no more walking around on the beach, no more selling postcard, no more tourist guide, just being in his house with him and going to school. He wants to send us to school like rich boys. He's not a tourist, he's living here all the time and wants to have us like we are his own boys."

"He's having a nice house. It's small but nice. Nice refrigerator. Big bed. Bathroom is there and tv. Compound is nice, mango trees, banana trees," said Modou noncommittally.

"He is a kind man and he is talking true," said Umaru.

"Yes, yes, but you know these men are all the same. They are nice because they want you to sleep with them. If you don't want to play some time they will be telling you bye-bye. Even Mr. James."

They lay quietly for a few minutes. Then Modou said, "But I am hearing you," and rolled over to face Umaru. "Just think about this: in even one month more we will have enough to be renting our own room and going to school. Just you and me together, we are buying what food we want, and we are having school uniforms and we are sitting at our table at night and studying our book. That's my dream, Umaru. Just you and me. Nobody is going to be saying 'come to bed now' or 'get up now' or 'go here now' or 'go buy some bread for me now.' I am saying, 'Umaru, you like some bread now?' and you are saying, 'Oh that is very sweet. Let me go and buy,' and I am saying, 'Oh no, let me go and buy. I am having money and you are my own small boy.' And we are sleeping in our one soft bed with sheet and fan and nobody is there but you and me." He laughed, "And maybe one nice girl sometimes."

"Mmm." Umaru nodded. "Yes, it's very good. I am having your dream now…nice book, nice pen, school crest on shirt pocket, school sandal, school shorts, underpants…"

"You want to be having underpants?"

"Mmm. Underpants are very necessary, for keeping penis from making bump in school shorts when he wants to stand up."

"Aha," agreed Modou. "You are very correct. We must be having underpants."

From: *The Masongala Daily Banner*

MCC Pleased with Vendor Registration Program
By Jason Andrews

Masongala City Council today received receipts and a report regarding the recent Street Vendor Licensing Bylaw. The report stated that about 800 vendors had been licensed to date and over K40,000 had been received in license fees. Councilors were unanimous in praising the results of the program. Councilor Abdou Jassy stated, "We now have control over the number of vendors and the ability to easily identify those who are not doing business in accordance with the laws. In addition, City Council now has a new source of revenue that we can use for improvements to the city infrastructure."

MCC Social Welfare Officer Mariama Dom said she was pleased that the age restrictions for licenses now means that there are only adult vendors in the streets and children will no longer be exploited by their parents to sell candy or cigarettes. Another councilor said that legitimate businessmen he had spoken to were unanimous in praise of council's action on this issue. He said, "Because each vendor is required to sign an agreement before receiving his license, we can now legally remove them from areas where they are in distracting shoppers from proper business establishments and shops." National Police Force of Dazania City Council Liason Officer Ebu Ndiaye added, "The National Police Force is pleased to have played an important role in initiating this program and we will be working hard to enforce it fully in the future."

Outside Council Chambers the streets of Masongala certainly look a little less congested than usual and the absence of child vendors is striking. However, not everyone is happy with the new bylaw. One street boy interviewed by this reporter said that because he was now too young to be a vendor he had no idea how he was going to support himself. He said, "Some boys, if they can't sell, will now be robbing. What else they go do? Everyone got to eat."

From: *The West Africa Intelligencer*

The Mysterious Toofas Coalition
By Rick Barry

Some call it the Toofas Coalition, some call it the Toofas Popular Front, and others refer to it as the Toofas Revolutionary Union. One hears these names whispered everywhere now in the streets and markets of Dazania's capital city Masongala. Yet it is impossible to find anyone who will talk openly about the underground movement that is opposed to the protracted rule of former military strong man President Yusufu Dafo.

Dafo was democratically elected three years ago after ruling as military dictator for several decades. However, during the election, one opposition candidate was assassinated and others were harassed and jailed on a variety of charges. Election results were described by international observers as "seriously flawed". Since then, opposition parties have been in disarray from fear of harassment by Dafo's secret police and also due to having widely divergent political views. Recently, however, the various opposition movements, recognizing their common need to oust Dafo from power, have apparently begun to hold secret meetings where they are planning a unified strategy. This is the most that anyone is willing to say about the Toofas movement.

Equally mysterious is the boy who has become a potent symbol of the opposition movement and has given his name to it. Since this reporter discovered that Toofas is the name of a street boy, he has been searching for this boy, so far without any success. His name has been adopted by the new political movement because of his spirit of independence and his remarkable ability to evade the entire national police force of this country. Street children here are routinely rounded up and relocated back to their home villages. But not Toofas. He always manages to slip through police drag nets and leave the officers dumbfounded and looking like fools.

Mention of his name brings a smile to most faces in the markets or streets but further questioning yields little information. People either do not know or are unwilling to say what has happened to him. Some fear he may have been "disappeared" like other political opponents of the Dafo regime but most are confident that the boy is simply too slippery for the police to catch. Rumour has it that a special reward has been offered to any police officer who succeeds in capturing the elusive urchin. The government, however, is clearly in a double bind. If Toofas is captured or killed he will become a martyr and an even more powerful figurehead for the growing opposition movement. But every day that the fleet-footed street kid remains at large the Dafo government looks more inept and impotent.

Twelve

It was late in the afternoon when Modou and Umaru left a cabana at the Kadanka Court Hotel.

"Thank you sir," said Modou. "We be seeing you tomorrow night."

As they strolled away they were discussing which food seller they would patronize for supper before they retired to their house. They made their way toward the beach but were alarmed at the edge of the hotel grounds by a shouted command for them to stop. One glance back told them that they needed to run.

The Anti-Exploitation detachment of police were making their first raid. "It's Toofas," cried one of the policemen swarming the grounds and cabanas of the hotel. The other officers immediately joined the pursuit. The Inspector-General had promised promotion to Sub-Inspector to any policeman who captured Toofas and the purpose for which they had come to the Kadanka Court was quickly forgotten when the name Toofas was heard.

The boys' initial adrenaline-fueled burst of speed had given them a good lead on the police but as they fled along the shore their pursuers remained uncomfortably close. Modou knew he could outrun them with ease but he had to run more slowly to stay with Umaru. At their current pace the police would eventually overtake them.

"Run away, Modou," panted Umaru. "They catch you, is serious. Me they only beat small small. Is no problem."

"No talking please," said Modou. "I am thinking."

Ahead they could see the Makalo Beach Bar. Modou's mind grappled with the layout of the hotel grounds behind the bar. There were a number of cabanas grouped around the swimming pool, then a large dining terrace and, he remembered glimpsing once, a long marble-floored hall-way that led right through the hotel to the lobby that faced Kadanka Bay Road.

"Just a little further, Umaru, and then we will be having a small rest," panted Modou. "Get ready to be making a turn. Soon we're going to visit some people in the Makalo Hotel."

"Toofas," yelled one of the policemen. "Stop now or we go shoot you!"

"Time to be running faster," said Modou and they accelerated.

A shot rang out but missed them. Two more shots whistled past their ears.

"Time to be visiting hotel, Umaru! Turn now!" hissed Modou and they abruptly changed direction and ran through the tables of the beach bar and into the hotel grounds. As they zigzagged between tourists lolling at poolside, the police charged into the grounds behind them, unable to shoot for fear of hitting one of the hotel guests, now scattering in dismay. The boys sped past the bathing-suited vacationers beside the pool and skittered around the bar at one end and onto the lawn. From there they leaped up onto the dining terrace and raced between the tables.

Modou tipped over several tables as he ran to slow the police and cause more confusion.

"Nice cake," he remarked and selected two pastries before he sent a dessert trolley careening down toward the policemen picking their way through disturbed diners and overturned tables. He slapped a twenty kuroma note down in front of the startled cashier as they left the dining area. "Two cake," he said. "Keep the change!"

"Umaru boy, now it's time to check out," he laughed as they powered down the long hallway that led through the center of the hotel, the stone tiles cool under their bare feet. In the lobby they rocketed through guests and staff and a newly arrived tour group milling around with their luggage carts. They spun through a revolving door to exit onto the plaza in front of the hotel.

"I am just moving your thing small small," said Modou as he pulled a baggage cart away from an astonished tourist. He rammed it into the still revolving door as it turned. It flipped over and jammed, locking the policemen inside the lobby.

"Umaru," giggled Modou as they ran across the parking lot toward Kadanka Bay Road. "This is no time for laughing. You must be breathing properly when you run. Running is serious business, you know."

By the time hotel staff had unblocked the door and police were able to exit the hotel, the boys were no longer visible. Heavily breathing police gathered with nearly hysterical hotel management in the plaza. A half dozen policemen wearing grim expressions peered up and down Kadanka Bay Road and wiped the sweat from their foreheads. Others assured worried hotel guests that there was no problem, nothing to worry about.

The Sub-Inspector in charge of the police at the Makalo Beach Hotel, determined to capture Toofas, telephoned for reinforcements from surrounding precincts. In a quarter of an hour he had arranged for an additional twenty police officers to carefully comb Casarica, to finally arrest Toofas. They sectioned the neighborhood and spread out, asking day guards and gardeners if they had seen two young boys.

When the boys were well within Casarica and no longer heard or saw any signs of pursuit, they slowed to a walk to regain their breath.

"Runners must be eating properly," said Modou offering one of the pastries to Umaru.

"Good cake," said Umaru as he licked the crumbs off his lips. "What're we going to do now?"

"These police are too troublesome. I think it's a good idea if we visit our friend Jason to rest with him small small. We will say we are just coming to take a bath. Maybe later the policemen will be going home."

As they walked down the road where Jason lived a security guard at a house they were passing hailed them, "You boys!"

"Salaam Alaikum, brother," said Modou

"Alaikum as-Salaam," said the guard. "What you boys do here walking around in Casarica?"

"Just go for visit our one friend, Mr. Jason. His house right there—you know, I think?"

"OK, OK. I hear someone shoot gun down for beach. Is some problem there?"

"We coming from Masongala, just now now," said Modou. "Bad thing, peoples shooting gun for beach. Is dangerous! Maybe we go back for Masongala soon soon."

Jason hummed while he fixed himself a ham sandwich.

He had just hung up the telephone after a long conversation with his former coach, Dan Brown. Dan was excited by Jason's letter and videotape and eager to begin training Modou. He had called in some favors and an American scholarship for the boy was right now being put together. Money was still a problem. Dan was scratching around to find enough for an air ticket but they had calculated that by the time Jason managed to get all the paperwork done, such as a passport and visa for Modou, Dan would have been able to secure funds sufficient for air fare and other costs. It might take them a couple of months to cross the finish line but the runners were now poised waiting for the starter's signal.

Another telephone call earlier in the day, from his overseas editor, had been both satisfying and frustrating. The Toofas story, which had been picked up by the wire services and widely featured in major newspapers, was still fresh in people's minds and his editor was eager to get another Toofas story. The internal politics of small African countries were usually lacking in human interest. The story of Toofas had jumped off the page and grabbed the attention of readers. If he could run the Toofas thing into a series, his editor said, his name would be made. Rick Barry was on the verge of fame and fortune and Jason would have been happy had he been able to locate the legendary Toofas. The boy had disappeared. The market people that Jason spoke to were clearly reluctant to talk about the boy or the underground movement he had inspired. When he had attempted to interview the police, they had become angry and suspicious.

Jason answered the knock on his door with a smile that broadened when he saw who it was. "Modou! And Umaru. Come in. Come in."

"Good afternoon, sir. We are coming for visit you. Is OK?" asked Modou.

"Yes, yes. It's fine." He led them into the kitchen. "I was just having a sandwich. Are you hungry?" He waved vaguely at the counter where the sandwich materials were laid out.

"What is that meat?" asked Modou. "Ham," said Jason. "Oh. Sorry, yes it's pig. But there's lots of bread and some peanut butter, some groundnut paste, if you like."

"We are running today, serious training," said Modou. Both boys looked sweaty and disheveled.

"Even Umaru?"

"Yes, Umaru is training today, running very fast," said Modou. Umaru blushed and Modou continued, "We like to be taking bath. We are very dirty. Is OK?"

"Yes, no problem. Go ahead. You know where everything is?"

"Yes, thank you. You are very good, sir."

Jason finished his sandwich and then went to the bathroom door. "Modou, can you come and talk to me for a few minutes, in the parlor?"

Modou came into the parlor wet and wearing just his shorts.

"I want to talk to you about your running."

"OK."

"Sit down. This is going to take a few minutes." They sat. "I'm really impressed by the way you run. I think you could be a champion, but you need expert training. I've been able to teach you a little but you need to be working with a real coach to put you into top form for competition."

"Thank you Jason, for thinking about me. Maybe you are knowing one coach?"

"Yes, I do, in America. He used to be my coach when I

ran for my college. He's very good and has trained athletes for the US Olympic team. I sent him your times and the video I took of you. He called me on the telephone today. He says he would like to train you."

Modou waited. Jason continued, "He's arranged a scholarship so you can go to America and live there. You can go to school and train with him. How does that sound?"

Modou was stunned. His eyes widened. "America, go to America. Oh Jason," said Modou slowly, his eyes sparkling. "Umaru and me in America."

"Actually," said Jason. "The scholarship is just for you. It's very expensive, you know, what with airfares and foreign student fees and your room and board and other costs, and the best we can do is to scrape up enough money for you to go. I'm afraid Umaru would have to stay here."

"We are not going together?"

"No, I'm afraid it's just for you. There's just not enough money for you both and no reason for anyone to give him a scholarship…" Jason stopped, shocked at the change in Modou's expression.

"Too bad," said Modou. "I am only going to any place with Umaru."

"Modou, please think about this," pleaded Jason.

Modou looked at him with a mixture of disgust and pity, and said, "No. I no go think like that, never."

Jason slumped back in his chair as if he had been hit. "I don't understand," he said.

"Yes, you are not understanding. Is a big mistake you make. Please don't ever be saying this to Umaru." Modou stood up. "We must go now and not trouble you any longer. Please give me our money."

Jason numbly went into his bedroom, unlocked the desk

drawer and removed the large envelope containing the boys'
money. Modou put it inside the waistband of his shorts.

"Modou, this is a once in a lifetime chance...."

Modou held up his hand. "No more talking, please. Is
an insult you are saying. Is bad for me to be hearing this."
He turned away then stopped and looked back. "I know is a
good thing you try to do but if Umaru knew this he would
just run away and die." He walked out and down the hall
toward the bathroom.

Jason turned and stared out his bedroom window.
His perplexity turned to alarm when his eyes were met by
those of a Dazanian police officer who walked up to the
window and looked back at him. Jason moved toward the
window but was suddenly gripped by both arms. Two
police officers held him. He heard a crash and the sound
of breaking glass from the bathroom. There were shouts
and the thud of running feet inside and outside the house.

A voice outside the house shouted, "Spread out, look
carefully, he can't have gone far."

Modou sat perfectly still, perched high in the dark
branches of an enormous mango tree several compounds
distant from Jason's. When the police had burst into the
bathroom, he had thrown himself against the window and
through the glass. He had landed on his shoulder on a shard
from the window. A long cut on his upper arm oozed blood
that trickled down and dripped off his elbow.

His worst wound was a deep slash on his thigh, received
when he broke through the glass. He held the wound closed
with his hand but it throbbed and leaked blood through his
fingers. He let go of the gash briefly to tear a long piece from
the bottom of his t-shirt. This he tightly wrapped around
his leg over the wound. The flow of blood slowed to an

ooze that reddened the makeshift bandage. He felt faint and grasped the trunk of the tree tightly. He closed his eyes and breathed deeply for a minute.

When he opened his eyes he looked carefully around. In addition to the police in Jason's compound, there were police in all the nearby streets and teams of them were entering each compound to search.

Modou waited silently in the mango tree. He knew he could not be seen from the ground. He watched Jason's compound until he saw Jason and Umaru come outside with police officers on each side of them. The police roughly pushed them into the back of a police van and it drove away. There was no longer any reason to remain where he was. Now he could make his move.

The sun was approaching the horizon as Modou stole carefully through the branches. His wounded leg had stiffened during his vigil in the treetop and he moved slowly until it loosened up and the pain subsided a little. He crawled like a chameleon along a branch that overhung the wall of the compound, lifting one limb at a time and pausing to look around. No police were visible so he swung down by his arms and dropped soundlessly into a crouch on the road. He trotted to the corner of the street, put his head around and peered up and down the wider street that connected to Kadanka Bay Road. It was clear so he crept through the shrubs that lined the street.

He was seen as he passed along the roadside. Two policemen raised a cry and the chase was on again. Sensing that his wounded leg was limiting not only his speed but also his endurance, Modou ran just fast enough to maintain his lead over the yelling policemen. Others, drawn by the shouting, joined the pursuit.

He crossed Kadanka Bay Road and sped up a pathway that wound through the forest to the beach. A dozen policemen surged after him. One sub-inspector remained at the foot of the path and directed carloads of police further down the road in both directions. They would try to box him in on the beach. Modou ran over the dunes, forcing himself to ignore the knifing pain in his leg. He relaxed during the downhill run to the shore, then accelerated as he turned toward Kadanka Point. It seemed further away than usual.

Kadanka Bay was bounded at this end of its curve by a high, boulder-strewn spit, Kadanka Point, that reached out into the ocean. Beyond this point was a short stretch of rocky undeveloped coast with an army barracks on top of a cliff above the beach. The far end of that rough shoreline of rocks and sand marked the beginning of the *bolong* that stretched all the way to Masongala.

Modou had continued to conserve his energy by simply maintaining his advantage, but he had to speed up when he saw policemen racing down the dunes on his right, to flank him. They failed to block him and joined the others chasing him along the shore. Other police continued to appear on the dunes ahead of him and he drew on his last reserves of strength to make it past them before they reached the shoreline. He neared Kadanka Point and raced up the incline to the path that led to the beach on the other side.

"Shoot!" cried a policeman. "He's getting away."

Several shots were fired as he gained the bush that covered Kadanka Point but none hit him. He raced across the flat top and down the far side of the point, then out onto the other beach. There he stopped. In front of him, holding their rifles nervously and looking suspiciously around, was a patrol of soldiers from the barracks above the beach. They had heard the shots fired by the police and were all turned facing Modou. They fingered their rifles uncertainly.

For a frozen second the soldiers and Modou stared at each other. Then Modou shouted, "Help!" and turned and ran back up the path towards the top of Kadanka Point.

"Stop!" ordered one of the soldiers but they all ran after him as he led them up onto the top of the point. The sun had nearly set by this time and the twilight made it difficult to see. The police officers coming up the other slope of the point began shooting as soon as they saw the boy. One bullet creased the side of his head and knocked him down. Another bullet passed him and went on to strike a soldier in the arm. The soldiers dropped to the ground and returned the policemen's fire and the police fired back in panic and fury. Both sides sought cover and continued shooting at their ambushers.

While the pitched battle raged, Modou wormed his way through the bush at ground level until he was well back of the point, then crept silently until he had passed the soldiers' position. A quarter of an hour later he had reached the edge of the bolong. He entered this dense mesh of roots, branches and mud with a sense of relief, but kept moving deeper into it for another quarter hour before he allowed himself to rest. His head ached and pounded from the bullet wound above his ear. He slumped in the mud and listened. A cloud of mosquitoes whined angrily around him and he felt the tiny pricks as they settled on him and drove their sharp needles into his skin. Their whining was punctuated by sharp bursts of gunfire from Kadanka Point. Modou made a noise that was both a laugh and a sob.

After a few minutes, he lifted himself up. He must find his way to the shore before the light failed completely or he would be lost in the swamp all night. He found the beach in a few minutes and began his trek toward the city. The moon rose and lighted his way.

Although he appeared to have lost his pursuers, he stayed watchful and wary. The only people likely to be out on this unpleasant strip of coastline at night were thieves. If they caught him they would most certainly rob him, but he could see well enough in the moonlight to spot danger, provided he stayed alert.

The mangrove thickets crept down to the water on much of this beach, leaving only a narrow strip where he could walk. Sometimes he had to wade out up to his knees to avoid the tangle of mangrove roots and his feet were bitten by the many small crabs that scavenged in the murky water. When he had to pick his way through the mangrove roots, the shells of the oysters that clustered there cut his shins and ankles. In other places the sand stretched back to form a real beach for fifty or a hundred meters before the encroaching mangroves forced him back down into the shallows. He saw a fire as he came to the edge of one of these small beaches and ducked down to watch and listen.

Moonlight silvered the sand for thirty meters up to where three men were gathered around the brilliant orange flames, drinking and talking. There were two options open to him. He could cut back into the swamp and circle widely around the men at the fire or he could make a run for it directly across the beach. They would almost certainly see him in the moonlight but would probably be unable to catch him. If he chose to circle around, it would take him several hours to work his way through the tangled web of roots and mud. If the men heard him, they might follow him into the swamp and it would be difficult to evade them in the darkness. They lived in this swamp and knew it well.

He decided to run and sprinted out into the open area. Almost immediately he heard a shout and the men started up from their fire and ran toward him. There was no more shouting. The thieves were intent on their prey and he heard the thud of their feet on the sand close behind. He remembered Jason's advice about not looking back and concentrated on running. By the time he reached the other side of the beach and darted along the narrow shelf beside the water, the sound of pursuit was falling away. When he was certain they had given up he slowed once again to a walk. He could no longer distinguish the pain of his leg wound. The entire leg was a single massive inflammation that shot a bolt of pain with each step, but he continued to march forward. There was nothing he could do until dawn but it would be less risky if he could reach his objective before the light of day brought watchers to the streets.

Thirteen

"Toofas boy! Aieee! You looking too bad. Come in quickly, come in."

Haruna Ceesay, "The Fixer", held open the door to his house so Modou could go inside. He and Modou were well acquainted from the days when Modou had run errands and carried messages in Manjako Market. Haruna was called "The Fixer" because he had extensive connections with the police. Two of his brothers were policemen, two cousins were Sub-Inspectors and his father-in-law was an Inspector. It was well known in the market that if you had trouble with the police, Haruna Ceesay was the man to see. Modou had carried messages for him many times and Haruna liked and trusted the boy. He took in the dried blood on Modou's head and his roughly bandaged leg and called to his wife, "Fatou!" When she came in he said, "Look this boy. Bring something for doctor him up while we talk. Bring bread and coffee first." He turned to Modou and pulled him towards a sofa. "You just sit there boy. Everything going to be OK. Just relax now."

Modou looked so battered, so young and helpless that Haruna's heart went out to him. He sat down beside the boy and put his arm around his shoulder. Modou collapsed against him and cried.

"Yes, yes, is fine," said Haruna encouragingly. "You been a big man too long. Sometimes is OK to be a small boy. Don't worry, you got some bad problem, I go fix it. Just now you go ahead and be small boy."

Fatou came in with two cups of coffee and buttered bread on a tray and set it down in front of them. She looked searchingly at Modou then went out and returned a few minutes later with a big basin of water and some cloths, bandages and a bottle of disinfectant. She squatted on the floor in front of Modou and waited until his sobs subsided.

Modou sat up, sniffled and wiped his eyes. "Oooh! Feeling much better now," he said with a sigh.

"Drink some coffee now," said Fatou, "and I go clean you up." She gently lifted one foot and began to bathe it.

"Oh, Ma," he protested. "Is too dirty."

"Drink coffee," she threatened. "I wash so many boys I forget them all. Is nothing to me, one more small dirty foot."

Modou turned to Haruna. "You know," he said with a shaky grin, "you should open one shop in market for peoples to come and cry on you. You expert! I feel too good now. Cry like that is worth even ten kuromas."

Haruna laughed and passed his hand across his eyes, "Is Toofas come back now. OK. OK. OK," he said hoarsely and cleared his throat. "Now let's talk about this bad problem you got, see how I can help you."

Fatou bathed and swabbed the grit out of the many small cuts and bandaged the worst of them while Modou ate his breakfast of bread and coffee. He told them how he and Umaru had fled from the police through the Makalo Beach

Hotel and about Jason and Umaru later being taken by the police. When he described the police and army battle at Kadanka Point, Haruna and his wife were speechless. Then Haruna laughed until he had to wipe his eyes.

"Oh Toofas! You are some boy!" he exclaimed.

"You're too much boy, I think," said Fatou but the harshness of her words was edged with wonder. "One day soon you go end up dead if you keep on like this."

Modou then explained that he wanted Haruna to see if he could get Jason and Umaru out of jail.

Haruna sat back and looked unhappy. "Is a bad problem. Is a *toubab* alongside Umaru. Going to be very cost. You got any money?"

Modou reached into his waistband and took out the envelope. He handed it to Haruna, who looked inside. "Kai! Is a lot of money. You been robbing bank?"

"No, we been selling, on beach, long time. This our savings, Umaru and me. Is all we have."

"How much?"

"Is six thousand four hundred kuromas."

"Maybe is enough. I go try. I go see my father-in-law, the Inspector, first. Maybe he go come with me. I go try." He looked at his wife and raised his eyebrows significantly. "Got to hide this boy. Maybe if you put him on one bed and cover him up with one sheet and he lie very still, no-one go see him."

Fatou nodded.

Haruna turned to Modou, "Going to take me two, maybe three hours. You wait here. OK?"

Modou was asleep even before Fatou pushed a pillow under his head and tucked the sheet around him. She sat down beside him and gently smoothed his brow. The worry lines melted from his face then and he fell into a deep untroubled sleep.

Modou came instantly awake as soon as he heard Haruna's voice in the house. He got up stiffly and went to greet him. They sat down on the sofa in Haruna's parlor.

"Toofas boy, I am having small good news but mostly bad news."

Modou waited in silence and Haruna continued, "Police did roundup in market this morning. They decide they have no use for Umaru so they put him on first police truck they sent north. Umaru no be for Masongala. He gone."

"Aieee," groaned Modou. He fingered the bandage on his leg and stared at the floor. Then he looked up. "Good news is?"

"Small good news. Police are very angry at this *toubab*. First they thought he was hiding you but it seems he don't know anything about Toofas. Then they are looking in his computer and finding he is writing bad things about Dazania but using another name. They want to punish him severely. But they are a little bit afraid to be beating him. Is not good to be beating men from big newspapers. They go let him go but it go be very cost and he must agree to be leaving Dazania now now, and not coming back."

"How much it go cost?"

"It go take all your money."

Modou nodded. "OK. Give money for let *toubab* go," he said. Then he set his jaw. "Time for me to go find Umaru now."

Haruna grabbed his shoulder as the boy rose to move toward the outside door. "Toofas, listen. Ten minutes no go make any difference," he smiled, "so at least sit down here with me and let us think about it together just a little." Modou nodded slowly and sat back down. Haruna called out, "Fatou, I am smelling your good oily rice cooking. Please bring two plates for hungry men."

While they ate the delicious spiced rice, Fatou left the house to buy some clean used clothes for Modou, a pair of plastic sandals and a small backpack to carry some food. After eating, he dressed in the clean clothes and returned to the parlor.

"How you go find him?" asked Haruna.

"Always I am telling him, if he is roundup, walk for main highway coming down to Masongala. He is there now. I will be walking main highway going up to meet him."

"Be careful, Toofas. Many police are remembering you. When you last left Manjako the police looked like fools and the peoples laughed them out of the market for many days. Even now, if market vendors want to tease the police, they will be singing, 'Toofas! Toofas! Toofas!' If police catch you, some of them, they go leave you alive only for beat you again and again. Many are saying they go break your legs into many pieces if they see you. I fear to speak your name to policemen even in my own family. If they catch you I no can help you at all at all."

Fatou came into the room and packed a loaf of bread, some hardboiled eggs, a tin of sardines and a bottle of water into the pack. She put it on his back and pressed a fifty-kuroma note into his hand. Lastly she carefully placed a baseball cap on his head to hide the graze of the bullet above his ear.

He stopped at the door and turned. "Salaam Alaikum, Haruna Ceesay, Salaam Alaikum, Mama Fatou."

"Alaikum as-Salaam!" they said together as he limped out into the morning sunlight.

Neatly dressed as he was and with his largest wounds safely under the cover of his fresh clothing, Modou risked riding in a minibus as far as the first town on the highway outside Masongala. The van was not stopped at any roadblock. He stepped down from the van at noon and began his walk northwards. Umaru would be somewhere along the highway. His leg pained him as he walked and his shoulder wound throbbed with its own rhythm. Under the burning mid-day sun, the side of his head ached where the police bullet had nicked him. The pains, however, kept his worries about Umaru at bay, though they filled his mind when he sat down to drink a little water and rest in midafternoon.

In the late afternoon he scanned the countryside ahead as he marched, looking for a compound where he might find shelter for the night.

⚜

Many of the street children in the police vehicle with Umaru had been dropped near their villages before the truck passed his family compound. Then it stopped outside a village nearby that he had identified as his home. The policemen pulled Umaru out of the back of the truck, hit him and kicked him a few times, then continued on their way. Umaru lay by the dusty roadside until he could no longer hear the truck. Then he dried his eyes and pulled himself to his feet. He remembered what Modou had said and set out to walk back to the city.

After walking for a half hour he saw his family compound. It was now in ruins. The rains had melted the mud walls and the thatched roofs had mouldered away. He looked at his former home once then kept his eyes on the road that lay ahead until he was well past and the tightness in his chest had lessened. The sun dropped lower in the sky as he trudged down the highway and he feared to face the night alone.

When it was nearly too dark to see his feet he spied the glow of a fire from a compound several hundred meters off the highway. He stumbled through the darkness until he reached the compound gate. Inside he could hear many voices talking and the sounds of children playing. He called a greeting and a small girl opened the gate.

"Ma, there is one boy here," she called over her shoulder.

A big woman came to the gate and held it open wider to see his face, then took his hand and pulled him inside. She sat him down by her cooking fire and started to ask him questions. Then she looked at his face and stopped.

"Aieee! I have such a big mouth. Asking foolish questions when I can see all I need to know. Here, eat this food. Later we can be talking if you like."

She gave him a big plate of rice and pulled him down beside her, all the while chattering and shouting to her children and other family members who moved in and out of the firelight. Umaru edged closer to her while he ate and only a few minutes after he had finished, he fell asleep against her warm broad shoulder and the plate dropped from his hands. The woman gently lifted him up and laid him down in her bed.

※

As the sun dipped below the horizon Modou saw a cluster of huts in the distance. In the last light of day he approached the compound gate and called a greeting. A man returned his greeting as he opened the gate. Modou asked to be allowed to rest in their compound overnight and the man assented and invited him inside. Soon he was gathered around a communal basin of rice with the men of the compound since he was a guest. A boy his age would normally eat with the children. When they had eaten their fill and washed their hands, the men, three brothers whose families shared this compound, asked him for news of Masongala and, more particularly, for news of Toofas. Stories of this boy had spread up into the rural areas and the people there had enjoyed them as much as their urban compatriots.

Modou said he knew nothing of Toofas. They were disappointed and shared the stories they had heard with him. Modou felt a little ashamed to be enjoying their company and their stories without revealing who he was but decided it was best if they thought he was only a boy passing through. The children in the compound gathered around the men and listened with wide eyes as Toofas' flight across the roofs of Manjako Market was described.

The compound gate opened and a boy came in. He and Modou recognized each other immediately. He was one of those boys who came and went in the market, working there when he was not needed on his father's compound. He and Modou had often spent time together in Manjako market.

He ran toward Modou and called, "Toofas!" with evident happiness at seeing his old friend.

Everyone gazed at Modou in wonder as he greeted the other boy. Questions flew and he had to confess that he was Toofas. He begged them to keep his identity a secret since both army and police were looking for him. They insisted he tell them about his flight through the Makalo Hotel and what was now being called the Battle of Kadanka Bay, since they had heard only the sketchiest accounts. They treated him as an honored guest and even the men of the compound sat at his feet and listened with awe and shouts of laughter as he described the events of the previous day.

When the children had begun to nod in the arms of their parents and big sisters and brothers, Modou was led to the bed in the largest house, usually occupied by the senior brother. He declined the offer with honest modesty, overwhelmed and uncomfortable with the adulation he was receiving. His hosts would not listen and insisted that he sleep in the best bed. They tucked the edges of the mosquito net carefully under the straw mattress after he curled up to sleep. He fell into a deep slumber almost immediately.

The adults of the compound gathered around the embers of the cooking fire and spoke of the boy in hushed tones so as not to disturb his sleep. He was so young and so modest they felt he was even greater than they had heard.

❦

When Umaru awoke in the morning and stepped out of the hut, the woman greeted him.

"Today I can see you," she said. "Are you feeling well, now?"

"Yes, Ma," said Umaru. "You are very kind. Thank you."

She called to a small boy, "Ahmadu, show this boy where he can wash. Then bring him back for some breakfast."

Umaru answered all her kind questions while he ate breakfast. He felt good in this compound. He imagined he could stay there and become one of the woman's children but as soon as he had that thought, another picture came to his mind. He saw Modou walking down the highway searching and never finding him. He knew in the same instant how he would feel if he were never to see Modou again.

He washed his plate and handed it to her. "Ma, I must go."

"Why go?" she said, because the boy had touched her heart. "Stay here with us even for a little while, until you are stronger."

"My friend is looking for me on the road. I must go."

She walked with him to the gate.

"Ma, Salaam Alaikum!" he said.

"Alaikum as-Salaam!" she replied.

All morning he walked and saw only one small van. He did not try to hitch a ride for fear he might be passed by Modou in a vehicle going the other way. He must walk until Modou found him. There were no villages or compounds. On both sides of the highway the flat land stretched away with only a few withered bushes and stunted trees to mark the distance.

When the sun was high overhead he heard a truck approaching behind him. He paused to look at it as it passed but it geared down and slowed to a stop beside him. It was piled so high with boxes and bales it looked as though it would tip over any minute. On top of the load were several passengers who looked down on him and smiled. The door of the truck opened and the trucker said, "What you doing here boy? Is nobody here. Get on truck now and we go carry you for Sandango Town."

"Thank you, sir," said Umaru, "but I must be walking to meet my friend. He is on this road coming to find me."

"Is a long way to walk," said the trucker.

"No problem," said Umaru, "but if you are having some water, I'm very thirsty."

The trucker gave him a half bottle of water. He carried on walking under the merciless sun.

In the late afternoon he suddenly glimpsed from the corner of his eye something moving. He looked but saw nothing and doggedly trudged on. A few minutes later he caught the movement again. He slid his eyes sideways then without turning his head and saw the hyena, trotting in its slope-shouldered way on a track parallel to his own, from bush to bush, about fifty meters away. He looked at it then and it turned its head sideways and emitted its bloodthirsty whimpering as it skipped lightly back.

He summoned all his courage and shouted fiercely and darted a few steps toward it. The hyena flinched and laughed crazily as it bounded away. But it stopped then and continued to stalk him as he moved along the highway, now and then whimpering and squealing hungrily and stretching its powerful jaws to reveal its sharp teeth. Each time Umaru looked at the hyena it leaped away, but each time it was closer and its cries became more anguished and insane.

Umaru drove it off repeatedly by throwing stones at it, but still it returned and sidled ever closer, howling and squealing when struck by a rock but not moving away. He realized it was only a matter of time before the beast overcame its fear and attacked him.

He spied a small tree a short distance away on the other side of the highway. When he was opposite the tree he bent over, selected a handful of rocks and pelted the hyena until it retreated. Then he raced across the highway to the tree and clambered up its trunk. The hyena snorted and whimpered and sped across the highway after him, reaching him just as he mounted the slender tree trunk. Umaru heard the click of the jaws snapping shut and dragged himself higher. His shorts seemed to be caught on something and he pulled free of them and up onto a higher branch. When he looked down, the hyena's head was entangled in his shorts. It threw itself about furiously, whipping its head back and forth and shrieking. When it had shaken the shorts free it tore them with its great teeth until they were in tattered strips. Then it returned to the tree.

Umaru was as high as he could go. The branches he rested on were bent beneath his weight and those above him would break if he tried to climb higher. The hyena pranced around the tree below him, looking up and making weak jumps. It put its front paws on the trunk and tried to pull itself up. It was unable to climb and circled the tree angrily at a greater distance. Then it ran toward him and gave a mighty leap. Umaru shrank back, only barely beyond the reach of the hyena's jaws. Three times more it took running leaps but each time its jagged teeth failed to reach Umaru's flesh.

The hyena seemed unable to keep still. It roamed from one side of the tree to the other and ran in its ugly sloping way from side to side, leering up at him and seeking some different way to attack. Darkness fell and Umaru could only sense where the hyena was by the crazed sounds it made as it restlessly circled the tree. It howled and laughed. Late in the night its calls were echoed by another hyena. The two squealed and fought but never left the vicinity of the tree where Umaru shivered and cried and prayed for the dawn.

He saw the headlights of an approaching vehicle growing larger in the darkness. When it was near he stood up in the tree, balancing precariously and holding gingerly onto the few small branches available. He waved with one hand and shouted as the truck roared past. But they did not see him. The red taillights grew smaller and smaller until they disappeared and he was left alone with the hyenas in the black night. They had retreated when the truck passed but now rushed back, giggling and grunting in frustration and insane delight.

※

In the morning Modou had arisen before it was light. The people of the compound gave him a good breakfast and begged him to stay with them at least until his wounds had healed. However, once they were convinced of the sincerity of his refusals they escorted him to the roadside and waved and shouted until he could no longer be seen.

He walked all day in the desolate landscape, ceaselessly searching ahead for Umaru's small figure. He passed through a region of rocky hills at dusk and found shelter in a jumble of boulders by the road. In his pack he found that Fatou had thoughtfully included some matches in a side pocket. He built a fire there and ate some of the bread that she had provided. It was dry and hard but tasted good. With a bright fire crackling before him and large boulders guarding his back he felt secure, but sleep did not come easily. He drifted in and out of dreams. Once he came completely awake suddenly and sat up and listened. There was no sound. Then he heard faintly the wild cackling of hunting hyenas, but it came from far away. He closed his eyes again and dozed restlessly until dawn.

The pair of hyenas besieging Umaru stopped making their noises with the first hint of dawn and as it grew lighter he began to hope they had moved on in search of other prey. But when it was light enough to see, he spotted first one, then the other, lying down, some distance away. Neither was sleeping. Though they rested quietly, they constantly turned their heads sideways and eyed the tree.

For an hour after dawn they were silent and watchful. Then the new hyena rose and bounded up to the tree to investigate. It was much larger than the first hyena and Umaru guessed it was a female from its size, though it otherwise looked the same as a male. It tried all the tricks of the first hyena, jumping up toward him and trying to pull itself up the trunk of the tree. Then it circled away and galloped toward him and vaulted into the tree. Its jaws locked on one of the branches where Umaru squatted in terror. He drove his heel into the animal's nose as it jerked and snarled and scrabbled with its claws against the trunk of the tree. Its weight and the power of its jaws crushed the limb and the hyena tumbled onto the ground, shrieking and crying with rage. It thrashed and snapped at the branch until it was in pieces.

Umaru stood up on the three remaining branches capable of bearing his weight and screamed, "Modou!" but the only answer was the mad wailing laughter of the hyenas. The larger one began circling the tree again, leering sideways at Umaru and backing up to gain distance for another running leap. Again it ran and sprang and seized another branch that broke beneath its weight and was destroyed in mindless fury. Now Umaru stood on two thin branches.

He heard the sound first, then far down the road he saw a truck approaching. The hyena, preparing to make another run, hesitated when it heard the sound of the motor. As the vehicle came nearer Umaru slipped out of his t-shirt and frantically waved it like a flag above the treetop while he shouted for help.

The truck geared down and halted just beside the tree and the driver looked at him through his open window. "Boy," he said, "what you doing naked in that tree?"

"*Mbarodi*," sobbed Umaru and pointed to where the hyenas glared warily at them from a safe distance.

The man glanced and then opened his door. "Ho, boy! You one lucky boy for sure. Jump down now and get in."

After taking an anxious look at the hyenas, Umaru jumped down from the tree and climbed up into the cab of the truck. He pulled on his t-shirt as the man reached past him to pull the door shut.

The man asked Umaru how he happened to get himself into such a situation. Umaru answered as best he could but after a few minutes the roar of the engine and the feeling of safety made him so sleepy he could hardly talk.

"Please, sir," he said, "I am looking for my one friend who is on this road. If you see one boy walking or running for road, please stop."

The trucker looked at him and said, "I go watch for you. Don't worry. If I see him I go stop."

Umaru went immediately to sleep and slept for a half hour before he was able to shake himself awake.

"Is nobody here on this highway," said the trucker. "I am not seeing your friend."

"Thank you sir," said Umaru. "How long before we go reach Masongala?"

The trucker laughed, "Masongala? This truck no go for Masongala." He pointed behind him with his thumb. "Masongala back there. This truck is go north."

Umaru sat in stunned silence. Then sat up straighter and squared his shoulders. "Please sir, now you be letting me get down."

"Here?" said the astonished trucker. "Is nothing here. Why you want to get down?"

"My friend is coming from Masongala, looking for me. I go meet him for road," said Umaru.

"You no fear *mbarodi*?"

"I go find one big stick," said Umaru firmly, though his lower lip quivered. "Please let me down."

The driver shook his head but began to gear down to slow the truck. "You one crazy boy," he said as he braked. The vehicle stopped and Umaru got out on the roadside.

"Thank you, sir," he said. The driver gave him a drink of water and then drove away. Umaru walked along the highway in the opposite direction, hoping fervently that the hyenas had gone away from the area.

⚹

In the morning Modou noticed that his leg and other wounds had begun to heal and he walked with less pain. With each passing hour, however, his worries for Umaru increased. He remembered his smile, the soft light in his eyes, and the joyous little songs he sang. He quickened his pace and peered hungrily into the distance every time he crested a small rise. In the afternoon he caught sight of a bit of color on the roadside near a small tree and crossed the highway to see what it was.

Modou picked up the shredded and torn shorts with a sinking heart and held them to his nose. He looked at them again and knew he was holding Umaru's shorts. He looked at the ground and saw the many hyena tracks, big ones and smaller ones. He looked up into the tree and saw the scars where the branches had been torn away. He circled around the tree and searched among the hyena tracks for any trace of Umaru's footprints, or any sign of the boy himself. He saw nothing that would tell him what had happened and he returned to stand under the tree. "Umaru!" he shouted, again and again. His voice disappeared in the vastness and there was no answer. He slumped down at the foot of the tree and buried his face in the tatters of cloth.

e-mail to: chuck@waintel.com
from: rbarry@hotmail.com
Hi Chuck,

I'm flying to London in a couple of hours. I've been in jail. A mysterious benefactor had me released earlier today but I've been declared a *persona non grata* by the government. Will explain all when I get there.

For now, I've attached a couple more Toofas stories.

Don't release the first until after 1600 hours GMT, today.

I'll be on the plane by then. I don't want to attract any more trouble before my departure.

Hold the second one until the first one is on the wires.

See you soon.

Jason

Battle at Makalo Beach – Toofas Wins Again
By Rick Barry

In Dazania's capitol, Masongala, the people are rejoicing over the latest exploit of the street kid who has won their hearts and inspired an underground opposition movement, the legendary Toofas, a boy as sharp as a tack and as elusive as the famed Scarlet Pimpernel.

Staff at the prestigious five star Makalo Beach Hotel are not so merry as they clean up the mess and repair the damage left behind when the wily urchin paid them a visit. When he passed through the hotel, "like a hurricane" said one staff member, he was being pursued by more than a dozen officers of the National Police Force of Dazania.

In the ensuing melee, tables were overturned and considerable damage was done in the Tiki Dining Lounge and in the lobby and entrance. What suffered most, however, was the hotel's reputation, since an incoming tour group cancelled on the spot and insisted on being accommodated elsewhere. Hotel officials were unable to provide specific figures but estimated that the total damages and lost revenues will exceed twenty thousand kuromas.

An NPFD spokesman said that Toofas is a dangerous criminal and must be apprehended before he endangers any more lives. The greatest danger these days in Masongala, however, is to be anywhere near an NPFD officer. The unrestrained laughter that meets their appearance on the streets draws a violent response and there are widespread reports of police brutality as the impotent officers vent their frustration.

In the next installment, read how Toofas offers the police a return engagement, tangles with a platoon of the Dazanian National Army and triumphs over both at the same time, single-handed.

Toofas Trounces Army, Police
By Rick Barry

Masongala, the capital of Dazania, is today abuzz with stories of a shootout between a rebel group being called the "Toofas Popular Front" and the national army and police forces near the famed Makalo tourist beach outside the city.

Police and army patrols were surprised by the sudden attack at the north end of Kadanka Bay, which resulted in one police officer's death and several wounded amongst both army and police forces. Casualties among the Toofas Popular Front (TPF), if any, appeared to have been carried off the field by their comrades since no bodies were found. A widespread rumor has it that the TPF insurgents were led by the legendary Toofas in person, fresh from his daring escape at the Makalo Beach Hotel.

Police and army spokesmen were unanimous in declaring that the group they surprised was no more than a large band of armed robbers and that they were successfully dispersed.

In the most spectacular popular version of what happened, there were no Toofas forces and it was Toofas alone who vanquished both the Dazania National Army and the Dazania National Police Force. This account is dismissed as mere mythmaking by some, but there's no denying that as the Toofas legend grows, opposition to the Dafo regime gains in strength and unity. Can one skinny street kid topple a government? It remains to be seen, but this observer's opinion is that the odds are in his favor.

Fourteen

Modou sat under the tree and wept, but after a few minutes he pushed the grief to the back of his mind, stood up and continued down the road. There was a slim chance that Umaru might have escaped, or he might be lying wounded somewhere nearby. He walked and he called to keep the immense weight of sorrow from crushing him to the ground. Without noticing, he began to run, slowly at first. Sadness hung over him like an immense cloud and he ran to escape it, grasping at the simpler pain from his wounds. He could feel the unbearable weight of grief just behind him and his legs pumped faster and faster. He ran and ran like never before, until he felt his heart was bursting. The wind tore Umaru's name from his lips and whipped the tears from his eyes, and then he saw a tiny figure moving in the far distance.

❧

After he had been dropped by the trucker and had started back along the road to Masongala, Umaru watched carefully for a big stick. He found one in mid morning and he walked more confidently. He paced steadily all morning and into the afternoon, seeking any sign of Modou on the narrow road that seemed to stretch endlessly ahead. His mind tormented him with thoughts of Modou being captured by the police or shot or beaten but he shook his head and stared into the distance. Modou would find him. He thought he heard a sound and looked ahead, squinting from the bright sunlight reflecting on the road surface. There, where the road waved and looked like water from the heat, he saw a small dot moving toward him. He walked more quickly. As the distant figure grew larger, he saw that it was racing and he knew it was Modou. He broke into a run.

When they met, they crashed together and fell to the ground and rolled over and over hugging one another. They laughed and cried until they were exhausted and then lay in the dust looking at each other with immense satisfaction.

In the shade of some large boulders they ate bread and tinned sardines from Modou's pack and exchanged stories of their adventures. Modou leaned back contentedly and looked up into the sky. Umaru followed his gaze. High overhead like a small bird a jet airliner crept across the sky.

Jason was pleased to find that his seatmate on the flight was Reba Brecken. While not close friends, they were well acquainted in the way that members of a small expatriate community often are. He looked out the oval window to the desolate brown landscape far below, tan colored and empty except for the few tiny dots of trees here and there.

"Are you going for home leave?" he asked.

"Business, all business," she replied, "though I expect to

enjoy it. First, I'm attending a conference in London. I've been asked to present a report on our work with Children in Difficult Circumstances in Dazania. It's received a lot of recognition and people are starting to look at it as a model of what can be achieved by a broad-based approach working simultaneously in multiple sectors." She smiled.

"That's quite a mouthful. What's after the conference?"

"Ah, that's the one I'm really looking forward to. I've got a promotion."

"Congratulations!"

"Yes, I'm really pumped—it's something I've wanted a long time. I'll be RKC coordinator for Africa, but first I have to spend about a month in New York familiarizing myself with larger issues and the various country programs."

"Fantastic. You must be very happy."

"I am, though I'm sorry to be leaving Dazania. It's been important to me. No matter where I go, I think my work will always be inspired by a little kid I met a couple of years ago on a field trip into the interior. He was the saddest little boy, and when I'm feeling doubtful or depressed, I just remember that my work freed him from what was really a kind of slavery and re-united him with his family."

"It must be wonderful to know you've accomplished something like that," said Jason.

"Well, it makes me thankful that I've had the opportunity. The memory of his face will always be an inspiration for me. His name was Modou."

"That's a coincidence. I was impressed by a kid there too, another Modou, but in my case it was a little bit of a disappointment."

"How so?" asked Reba.

"This kid was a natural athlete, a born runner, fastest

kid I ever saw, and I hustled an athletic scholarship for him at an American high school."

"Sounds good. What happened?"

"I don't really understand, but he funked it. Maybe it was too much pressure or something, I don't know. He just walked away from it." Jason shrugged his shoulders.

"What a shame. But don't feel bad. It often happens that you offer an opportunity, a chance for them to make something of themselves, and they can't cope with it."

"I suppose so," said Jason, "but you know what I regret most about leaving Dazania?"

"What?"

"This kid called Toofas. I really wish I could have found out a little more about him."

"Ah, the famous Toofas," said Reba knowingly.

"You know him?"

"No, but he's a street child you know, so one of my staff got very interested in finding out about him. We thought maybe we could make a case study of him if we could find him and work with him."

"And?"

"My staffer spent a lot of time in the market interviewing people about Toofas, you know, trying to locate him. He was never able to contact him, but maybe I can tell you a little about him."

"Please," said Jason as he extracted his notebook from his carry-on bag.

"It's probably just stuff you know already," she said.

"No, go ahead, anything about this kid is interesting."

"Well, apparently he's only about thirteen or fourteen years old. I had thought somehow that he was probably older, you know maybe sixteen or seventeen, the way people talk about him. He's supposed to be a good-looking boy and knew the market inside out, was always racing around carrying messages and making deliveries. Toofas was just a nickname. His real name, and here's a coincidence," she laughed, "his real name was Modou. Another Modou for our collection!" She laughed again. "Not much news there, I suppose. But there was something else about him that I never saw in any of the other reports. People in the market who knew him said that he was always with another kid, a smaller boy, and the two of them were inseparable," she laughed again, "like Batman and Robin."

Jason felt a cold wave of dismay slowly moving through him as if he were going to be sick. "What was the smaller boy's name?" he asked.

"Let me think," she pondered, then said triumphantly, "Umaru."

⁊

Umaru stared idly up into the blue sky and traced the flight of the jet with his finger. "What're we going to do now?" he asked.

"Plan B," said Modou.

"What's that?"

"You know, plan A is what you want to happen. When things go wrong, then you go to plan B."

"You got one plan B?"

"Ahuh! Plan B, we go for soldier boys. I've been hearing of one army, up north far far, they like to have boys come for join their army."

"But army is after you too, like police. You too popular."

"Not this army. This one is rebel army. Going to beat those Dafo soldiers down seriously."

"You think rebel army go give me some shorts? I got no shorts now."

"No problem," said Modou stroking his chin. "We'll just say, 'You giving shorts to soldier boys?' The army man, he is saying, 'Got two shorts for every boy,' and we say, 'OK, bring shorts, bring guns, we're coming in now now!'"

"It's good," said Umaru. "Let us go now."

ACKNOWLEGEMENTS:

Thanks to all who read and commented on the manuscript of this book. What you said and sometimes, what you didn't say, helped to give this book its final shape. Special thanks to my brother and my daughter for their enthusiasm for my writing and for their ongoing support. Thanks also to my editor, Ron Smith, for his insightful suggestions. Finally, thanks to all the street children who generously shared their lives with me and told me their stories. Without them I could not have written this book.

ABOUT THE AUTHOR

Trained as an anthropologist, Benjamin Madison lived and worked in West Africa for seventeen years, generally working in Education and Development. He lived for several years as a volunteer teacher in rural communities such as those featured in his remarkable collection of stories, *The Moon's Fireflies* (2010).

Benjamin Madison now resides in Victoria.